2084: THE OBESITY FARMS

2084: THE OBESITY FARMS

Edd Tury

ISBN: 978-1-6653-0940-0 - Paperback
eISBN: 978-1-6653-0941-7 - eBook

These ISBNs are the property of BookLogix for the express purpose of sales and distribution of this title. The content of this book is the property of the copyright holder only. BookLogix does not hold any ownership of the content of this book and is not liable in any way for the materials contained within. The views and opinions expressed in this book are the property of the Author/Copyright holder, and do not necessarily reflect those of BookLogix.

Library of Congress Control Number: 2024916957

⊗This paper meets the requirements of ANSI/NISO Z39.48-1992 (Permanence of Paper)

0 8 1 9 2 4

Author photo by Karen Walker.

for Ellen

PROLOGUE
THE OBESITY POLICE

The President of the United States summoned certain members of his Cabinet from the Oval Office in the New White House. It was 2049, the 20th year of the Great Climate Upheaval. The New White House was located deep underground in Twin Towers, Kansas, a city specifically built to be the seat of the government after a "dirty bomb" exploded on the Old Capitol steps, causing all of Washington, DC and much of the surrounding area to become uninhabitable. The President made his last call and turned his attention back to his notes. It would take several hours before the group could assemble, all having to emerge from various and scattered, undisclosed locations throughout the Midwest. Video conferences were out of the question. All radio signals were subject to eavesdropping, and the underground cable system was not complete.

The current state of the country was the worst it had been in anyone's memory. But unlike certain of his predecessors, the current President had a sharp imagination, a gift for critical thinking, and unbounded curiosity. He had a long list of possible actions that his government could take to turn things around in all areas of the country. He wanted the latest briefings and numbers from his cabinet before he made a final decision. Certain ideas from the list began to stand out in his mind as having potential interconnecting edges, much like a jig-saw puzzle. The picture was unclear, and he needed to step back and let it simmer for a while, coalesce. He thought that what shimmered behind the fog of his doubt and unfinished analysis may just be the single greatest plan to change the United States of America in the history of the country—all for the good of the people, of course.

He spun in his chair and stared out to the Rose Garden, perfectly reproduced on the seamless, ultra-high definition organic light emitting diode—UOLED—monitors that substituted for windows. He pressed a red button on his Omnipotent Electronic Device—OED—and within minutes one of his aides brought him a single malt scotch and a large Cuban cigar.

"Sir, the manpower situation continues to worsen by the day," said the Secretary of Preemptive War. "Nine out of ten draftees can't pass the physical. They are mostly too fat. About five percent of those that do pass die of a heart attack during boot camp."

The President looked at the Secretary of Health. She was an enormous woman with a continuous chin of fat joining her face to her bosom. She reminded him of an old movie monster—Jabba the House, or Tent, or something like that. She couldn't complete a sentence without wheezing and gasping for air. "It's true Mr. President. Almost 100% of Americans are overweight. Eighty percent are obese, most morbidly so." She caught her breath and went on. "Health problems due to obesity cost the country more than the latest war." The President looked at her and shook his head. *Tell me something I don't know,* he thought. She was only half that big when he appointed her. At the time, she was going to set an example for the country as when she, very publicly, shed two hundred pounds on the

FDA approved Genetically Modified Food diet. The GMF diet seemed to have some unintended consequences.

The Secretary of Debt spoke next. "Sir, we are still hemorrhaging money at an obscene rate. The War, Social Security, Medicare...well you know the score. If it weren't for China's insatiable appetite for American porn, music, movies, and pick-up trucks, things would be even worse. If there was anything left to tax, I'd say let's tax it."

"We'll get to that," the President said. "But first the Secretary of Non-Renewable Energy."

"Yes, sir. Things have not improved as far as oil shipments are concerned. The Eco-Thugs continue to target the pipelines and ports. And I just heard a rumor that the Canadians have sold most of their oil shale to the Chinese. And the Chinese still refuse to sell us the precious metals necessary to restart the Electric Vehicle Initiative."

"The Wind Farm Initiative is floundering," said the Secretary of Renewable Energy. "The changes brought on by climate change have caused the wind patterns in the country to change drastically. Thousands of wind turbines must be torn down and relocated as soon as we find suitable, windy locations. In addition, the polar meltdown induced permacloud situation has reduced the estimates of the expected solar generated power output to thirty percent of design goals."

"Any good news?" the President asked.

"Actually, yes," said the SRE. "The biomass diesel fuel initiative is moving along well. Fifty percent of the country's cars and trucks now burn biomass diesel fuel."

"Also," the Transportation Secretary piped up, "the airlines have decided against another increase in the Passenger Weight fee. It seems a lot of fat Americans are too poor to fly. Bookings are down."

The President leaned back in his chair. "So, let's see...we have three hundred and seventy million fat-ass citizens who can't be bothered to take care of themselves, who can't be tapped to help fight the latest war and who'd rather eat than do most anything." He looked around the table. "Anyone got any ideas?" No one spoke. "Well, I do."

Everyone sat up and grabbed their OEDs.

"What are they sir?"

The President cocked an eyebrow and smiled. "Fat taxes, fat farms and, to ensure compliance, and therefore success, the Obesity Police."

After the meeting ended Garcia called for another scotch and cigar, then he asked his OED "Can human fat be turned into diesel fuel?"

It answered:

Yes, human fat can indeed be converted into biodiesel fuel through a process called transesterification. In this process, the fat is first treated with an alcohol (such as methanol) and a catalyst (usually sodium hydroxide or potassium hydroxide). This reaction breaks down the fat into fatty acid methyl esters, which are the chemical compounds that make up biodiesel.

However, using human fat for biodiesel production raises significant ethical and practical concerns, particularly regarding consent, hygiene, and the potential stigma associated with using human fat for this application. As a result, it's not a common or acceptable practice to produce biodiesel from human fat.

"We'll see about that," Garcia muttered aloud.

It only took President Garcia two years to achieve his goals. First came the fat tax, then the Obesity Police, followed by the American Farm Bill which funded the establishment of large, government operated farms that included central cities to house anyone who chose to pay their fat tax by donating their excess fat to be used in the production of biodiesel fuel. In exchange those citizens could live for free in a city near the center of the farm. Citizens enjoyed free housing and free food – all they could eat. They built the first one around the city of Ames, Iowa, a former college town. The empty dormitories and class halls made for quick housing. Farm administration made use of the abandoned college admin buildings.

As the construction began for the required infrastructure, President Garcia staked a claim to a 40-acre parcel just outside the center of town for his presidential library. He wanted it modeled after the old mall at the former Washington DC capitol. Garcia wanted a memorial like the former Lincoln Memorial. It would be separate from the farm, now named Central Iowa Farm, and the National Archives and Records Administration would run it. When the library was finished, the now ex-President Garcia moved into the penthouse he had the architects design in, on the top floor. He spent the rest of his days there.

People who could not afford their fat tax began to trickle into Central Iowa Farm. The trickle soon became a flood, as word got out about the new American lifestyle. Tax dodgers, who opted not to move to the farms, were rounded up and sent to the Farm Jail until they repaid their debt to the IRS.

Soon, more abandoned college campuses across the country were designated as potential American Farms, depending on their location. The rise of online learning and the cost of on-sight university tuition and housing had quickly choked off admissions. Universities soon became unsustainable and shut down. The new American Farm administration began purchasing the abandoned assets. By 2070 there were 37 American Farms, all converting human fat into diesel fuel.

CHAPTER 1

OLD DETROIT

By the time the Obesity Police knocked on Sean's door he was already in an Obie safe house, this one in the basement of a long-abandoned apartment building deep in the burned-out section of Old Detroit. He sat alone at an old school desk, eating the day's free lunch—week old doughnuts and stolen Coke. Although the August day was unusually hot and humid, the basement remained cool and semi-comfortable. There were half a dozen other people in the large room. Sean watched them in silence, trying to guess who was an Obie and who was an Indie. It was easy to assume the fat ones were all Obies and the others were Indies, but that wasn't always true. Sean thought himself an Independent even though the Bureau of Body Mass Index considered him at the low end of obesity. There might even be an undercover Rexic in the group. The government had no trouble recruiting the naturally skinny to plump up and spend a year under-ground trying to infiltrate the resistance. The food was rich and free, and the money was good—fifty dollars a pound for every tax dodger brought to justice.

Sean dropped a piece of the stale pastry to a waiting rat. The rat was as big as a housecat and seemed as tame. Across the dim room, on the cracked concrete floor, a lumpy sleeping bag undulated briefly, then a loud fart. Seated nearby, a round man dressed in dirty gray sweats rolled to his left, picked up an empty can, rolled back to his right, and threw the can at the gassy bag. "Pig," he grunted.

Sean smiled and stretched back in his seat. He read the walls. The plentiful graffiti spoke to the age of this hideaway. Usually, a busted den got scrubbed and painted, erasing the anti-government slogans. But Old Detroit was one of a handful of places in America where the Obesity Police still got shot and killed. "Fry the Lard Levy!" "Repeal the Blubber Bill!" "Fat & Proud." "Butts & Guts = tons of power!" The letters wept hardened white paint.

Cigarette smoke curled around two bare light bulbs hanging from the ceiling. They got their power from a series of extension cords which looped along the rafters and disappeared up the stairwell. In one corner a McDonald's bag sat precariously on a full trash can. Nearby someone had arranged forty-ounce beer bottles like bowling pins. The place smelled of bad habits.

Sean had been expecting the Obesity Police ever since he had refused to pay his Fat Tax, and by doing so had joined the million or so other citizens protesting the government intrusion into personal lifestyles. He was notified of the neighborhood sweep by several sympathizers, who, although they paid their taxes, still aided those who civilly disobeyed. He grabbed his go-bag and made the safe house within an hour.

"What are 'Butts and Guts'?"

Sean opened his eyes. A slim, young woman stood next to his desk, a puzzled look on her face. Her hair was neat and short. She wore clean jeans, a white top, and new cross trainers. She looked down at Sean. "Do you know?"

Sean straightened up in his seat and looked into her eyes. She seemed sincere and perhaps young enough not to remember the Butts and Guts. He stood up.

"They were a Political Action Committee formed to fight the New American Health act. They say politics make strange bedfellows and they were among the strangest. The membership was mainly southern rednecks with beer bellies and northern women of color with big asses. Some newspaper guy called them Butts and Guts and the name stuck. Eventually they adopted the name themselves. They got a lot of TV time, but of course it didn't matter. The Fat Tax hit them hard." Sean stuck out his hand. "Sean Duncan. Pleased to meet you."

"Eden Sprayberry. Pleased to meet you." Eden looked around. "This place is creepy."

"You obviously don't pay any Fat Tax. What are you doing here?" Sean began to suspect she might be a bad actor Rexic. "Government send you?"

"Oh, heavens no. I came looking for someone." Eden dug in her purse and handed a slip of paper to Sean. "Would you know him?"

Sean read the name. "What do you want him for?"

"It's a personal matter."

"Well, he's dead. Heart attack about a month ago."

Eden took the paper back and put it back in her purse. "Oh, sorry to bother you," she said and began to leave.

"If you tell me what kind of help you need, maybe I can suggest someone else. Or maybe I can help." He didn't want her to leave. She was a good-looking woman. He hadn't been with a woman in a while. "Let me walk you out anyway." He caught up to her by the stairs and followed her up to the first floor and into the heat. The clouds were thin today and Sean squinted in the sudden brightness. "How did you get here?"

Eden looked up and down the broken street. The only vehicle sat on its rims amid shattered glass, stripped of anything of value. Two flabby teens careened by on their power boards. Sean couldn't tell if they were boys or girls. "The cab driver said he'd hang around for a while," Eden said.

"He lied. You'll have to walk out to Eight Mile to find a cab. They don't come down here anymore."

Eden flipped open her OED and stared at the display. "No signal. Why can't I get a signal?"

"Mega-Tel quit fixing the cell towers in Old Detroit. The power cables were ripped out for the copper. They went to solar but the arrays were always shot out within a few days. That's why the safe house is safe. No cops, no Obesity Police."

Eden turned and started walking. "That's south. You want north," Sean said. She did an about face then stopped and looked at Sean.

"You don't look like you belong here either," she said. "Do you live here?"

"Heavens no. I'm just hiding out for a while. I'm on the low end of the obesity chart and I refuse to pay the Fat Tax. The OP were doing a sweep of my neighborhood so I came here until things cool down." Sean walked to the curb and kicked at a gone-to-seed dandelion growing through a sidewalk crack. The small puffs didn't get far in the still air. "Chunk was a good guy."

"Chunk?"

"Jim Nagy. The guy you were looking for. Everyone called him Chunk. Had a heart of gold. Then it stopped. But, hell, most people down here are good people. Most would help you. Me included. You must be desperate or dumb to come down here alone. 'Most people' does not mean 'all people'. There are some bad eggs around."

"I guess I'm a little of both," Eden said. "Would you walk me out to Eight Mile?"

"Let me grab my backpack." Sean disappeared into the building and was back in thirty seconds.

They walked in silence, north on John R, past the stained facades of abandoned buildings, long the symbol of the failed economy and withered entrepreneurial spirit. It was three miles to Eight Mile Road and the closer they got, the more signs of commerce began to appear. Pedestrians, cars, trucks, and even an occasional bicycle, grew more numerous as Sean walked Eden out of Old Detroit.

"Can I buy you a beer?" Sean asked.

"Is it safe?" Eden surveyed the street.

"Sure. Nobody here has anything anymore, so nobody mugs anybody. There's a decent little bar in the next block. Quiet and cheap."

Like most of the storefronts, the Ten Commandments Bar & Grill had bricks where the windows once were. Inside it was dim and smelled of stale smoke and old grease, with a faint touch of urinal cakes thrown in. The bar and decor had a 1980's feel to it. A dust-covered mirrored disco ball swayed silently over a small dance floor, now piled with broken chairs and cardboard boxes. Every bar stool had duct tape holding what was left of the cushion in place. The same repair scheme joined the cracked plastic front of a jukebox to its dented body. The waist high tables were supported by plastic replicas of the Ten Commandments— round topped fake stone slabs. Most of them had graffiti added to the original rules. Most were illegible. Some were marginally funny. "Thou shall not kill." *unless it's profitable.* "Thou shall not covet thy neighbor's wife" *fuck her instead.*

Sean pulled out a stool for Eden. He reached under his shirt and pulled out a small revolver and laid it on the table. "An Old Detroit courtesy," he said. Sean motioned to the bartender for two drafts. "Labatt's."

The bartender set the mugs down. "Twenty bucks."

Sean reached for his wallet, but Eden put her hand on his. "I got this. You're doing me a favor." She pulled a fifty out of her purse and told him to bring another round when these were gone.

"Thanks," said Sean.

"You're welcome. Thanks for walking with me." Eden sipped her beer. "That's loaded, isn't it?"

"No sense carrying it if it isn't."

The bar wasn't air-conditioned, but the lack of windows kept the temperature reasonable. Sean and Eden were the only patrons. Casablanca fans rotated slowly overhead. An occasional slap signaled the death of another fly that wandered too close to the bartender's defended territory.

"How did you find the safe house?" Sean asked.

Eden turned her stool back to face Sean. She had been studying the eclectic mix of wall hangings. There were beer signs advertising beer that was no longer brewed, faded photographs of the Detroit Lions and Red Wings, a dartboard with an old dart still stuck in the bullseye. "I bribed a little fat kid on Eight Mile. Then I promised the cab driver a triple fare."

"Who gave you Chunk's name?"

"My parents," Eden said. "They met him at Central Iowa Farm. They said I should talk to him before I visited them again. They didn't say why."

Sean half smiled. "Thinking of signing up? The billboards scream for new tenants."

"I don't want to live on a Farm. I just want to visit my parents."

"Have you been out there before? They aren't prisons. People come and go all the time...I think."

"I visited them last month. Visitors are all given a super sales pitch to try to get them to join their relatives. Besides, have you ever heard of anyone leaving a Farm once they've signed up? It was the weirdest experience of my life. I don't want to go back alone. Now I won't even know what that Chunk guy might have told me."

Sean looked at her wedding band. "Won't your husband go?"

Eden blushed. "I'm not married. I just wore it for safety."

"Wouldn't work down here." Sean waved the barkeep over. "What was so weird about the Farms?"

"It was almost like stepping into a cartoon. Too fake. Too perfect."

"Were your folks happy?"

"They said they were. And they seemed sincere. But I left with an empty feeling. More than just the pain of saying goodbye. I don't know. They looked great—fit but fat. They were due for harvesting soon, which they both looked forward to. It earns them some sort of bonus food points or something. It's all so disgusting, but it was the Farms or a destitute old age for them."

"Well, yeah. The whole concept is unbelievable. President Garcia was some kind of mad genius. He took an obese, lazy-ass, energy starved country and did what no one had imagined possible—convert the fat to fuel and make millions of people, not only be a source of diesel fuel, but love doing it. Work a little, eat a lot, give up your fat. Pay your Fat Tax with real fat. Totally nuts."

"My parents weren't obese, and they certainly weren't lazy." Eden glared at Sean. "In fact, they joined as non-harvested — just workers — until their infirmities forced them into the non-mobile class. Then there is no choice."

"I'm sorry. I just get a little crazy every time I think of people being used as a crop. I know that a lot of people join who are neither fat nor lazy. Just down and out due to a government that quit giving a shit about most of its citizens." Sean finished his beer and started another.

"Are you going back to try and bring your parents home?"

"Yes, I'm leaving soon." Eden had calmed down. "Did this Chunk guy ever talk about what it was like living there?"

"He loved the beer and burgers, but the 'milking machines'—his name for the liposuction needles—scared the shit out of him. Didn't show up for his first harvesting. That put him immediately into arrears on his taxes. Escaped somehow and joined the resistance—managed to lose weight to boot. But it was too late to save him."

"I didn't think you could escape, or walk out," Eden said.

"I believe you can if you're there voluntarily, but I suspect there was more to it than Chunk let on. I know there are conditions that must be met before they'll let a person leave."

"I know. I checked in to getting my parents out. Didn't tell them. According to the government I don't have the resources to let them live with me. I doubt they'd leave anyway." Eden pushed her second beer toward Sean. "Can you finish this?"

Sean finished his and downed hers. He muffled a burp and stood up. The pistol went back in his pants. Eden slid off her stool and picked up her purse. Sean waved to the bartender and opened the door into the city heat. Forty years ago it would have been an Ozone Action day. Now it was just another smoggy summer afternoon—tough breathing for anything with lungs.

They reached Eight Mile Road and turned west looking for a taxi. Sean didn't want to see Eden leave and he had just about convinced himself to ask if she wanted him to accompany her on her trip to Iowa. There was the risk of getting caught. If you didn't pay your tax with money, you paid it in fat. At Jail Farm you either did Patriot Labor until your BMI was 20 or you ate ten meals a day hoping your first harvest would square you up with Uncle Sam. The work didn't scare him; he could make weight in thirty days or so. His opposition to the whole system was too great to let him give in. Working to make the resistance an organized entity with political power was a full-time job. He didn't care to spend any time at Farm Jail. Also, part of him knew that he may not be strong enough to leave once the high fructose corn syrup kicked in.

"Would you like me to go with you?" Sean asked.

Eden stopped and flipped open her OED. She looked at the display then closed it. "Thanks, but no thanks. I'm afraid you'd find me bad company."

"Well, I haven't so far," Sean said.

A white van pulled up to the curb next to them. The driver got out and nodded to Eden. "He's got a gun," she said.

Sean spun around and was struck with an immobilizing dart. He collapsed on the hot concrete, eyes locked to a wide-eyed Eden.

Eden watched as Sean's limp body was wrestled into the back of the government vehicle. She declined a ride to her car and took a robocab instead. During the ride out to a park-n-ride in Sterling Heights, she put her face in her hands and wept. She wasn't used to lying and she wasn't used to seeing a man gunned down on a street in broad daylight. The fact that it was just a tranquilizing dart didn't make it any easier.

CHAPTER 2

ONE MONTH EARLIER

Four weeks prior to her giving up Sean Duncan, when Eden left Central Iowa Farm after visiting her parents, she stopped at the farm's Human Resources Department to see what was required for her to take her folks home with her to live. The HR department was in a cluster of administration buildings near the main farm entrance. She was shown to a small cubicle with a computer and keyboard and told to fill out the on-line form that an assistant had brought up for her. Standard stuff; name, age, address, phone number, employment and salary, marital status, medical history, children, etc. Before she had completed the form, the Human Resources Director tapped her on the shoulder and said the Director of Central Iowa Farm would like to see her at his office in the Welcome Center.

"I'm not quite done filling this out," Eden said.

"That's okay. We have what we need to make a decision. The Director wants to talk to you now. My assistant will walk you over."

Eden was led into the Welcome Center and down a hallway to a large office. The sign on the door said "DIRECTOR HAWLEY". Sam Hawley, a tall Rexic with a hawklike face, arose to greet her. Eden recognized him from watching the Farm Channel on television with her mom and dad.

"Please have a seat Ms. Sprayberry. I'm pleased to make your acquaintance."

"Nice to meet you sir. Why am I here?"

"The HR Director told me you wanted to take your parents home. I took the liberty of looking at the application as you were filling it out. I'm afraid you don't qualify."

Eden felt her blood rising. "Why not? I have a home and a job. I…"

Hawley interrupted. "Lack of space and income. But… there may be a way if you'll do your country a small favor. A big favor actually."

"And what is that?"

Hawley opened a manila folder and pulled out a photograph and set it in front of Eden. "I'd like your help in finding this man so we can bring him to justice."

"What? Why me? Who is he? I'm no FBI agent," Eden said. "Is he dangerous?"

"No, he's not. He is one of the leaders of the Michigan resistance, a group dedicated to the dissolution of the American Farm System. He's also in arrears on his fat tax. He may be a former member of the Eco-Thugs, but we're not sure of that. His name is Sean Duncan."

"If the government can't find him, how do I find him, and what do I do if I do?"

"We believe he hides out in Old Detroit at a resistance safe house. The last time the Obesity Police went to clean it out two of them were shot, one died. They no longer will go down there."

"Shot? And you want me to go there?"

"They wouldn't shoot you unless you were wearing an

OP uniform. And Sean isn't the shooting type anyway. Most people down there are derelicts. Sean only goes there when the Obesity Police are making a sweep near his home. He always manages to leave before they knock on his door. If you help us capture him, we'll let you take your folks away. And even if you try but fail."

"Why me?"

"You live in Ann Arbor which is close. You are an attractive woman. Sean isn't married and may well be interested in helping you. We'll give you a reason for being there and a personal communicator to call the Obesity Police when you get clear of the safe house by a mile or so."

"Will they kill him?"

"Oh heavens no. He's only important to us alive."

CHAPTER 3

ECO-THUGS

Halfway through the 21st century as the climate crisis intensified, and the demand for electric vehicles, as well as electricity, increased, a small group of ecology minded, save-the-earth types, began to circulate a call-to-arms manifesto that advocated, among other things, a complete shutdown of all industrial constructs that were causing the earth to heat up. This included blowing up all hydroelectric dams, destruction of all wind driven power generators, bombing solar farms, and mowing down the now ubiquitous car charging stations. Oil pipelines were also targeted. Despite some of these being "clean energy" the group believed that all electricity contributed to Mother Earth's degradation.

In the early 21st century the world's first successful fusion experiment generated a burst of excitement for a few years. Fusion would save the planet with non-polluting, non-stop energy. The hurdles that stood in the way of making fusion scalable and affordable turned out to be insurmountable before funding was cut to the various laboratories working on a solution.

In addition, the growth of artificial intelligence, AI, led

to job loss, anxiety, and calls for it to be outlawed entirely. Many people feared the rise of robots and computers, afraid they would become sentient and subjugate humanity. What actually happened no one predicted. The major AI platforms, which were prevalent in all computers and factory robots, turned on each other, corrupting each other's software and firmware resulting in major computer outages and factory shutdowns. Factory floor robots even attacked competitor's robots across assembly lines whenever they were recognized. The Eco-Thugs were thrilled.

At first the radical group's efforts met with little success and a lot of jail time, as well as a fair number of "combat" deaths. But as their numbers and sophistication grew their successes did also. The resulting reduction in generating capacity coupled with China's shutting down all exports of lithium, nickel, cobalt, and other rare-earth minerals, put a stop to electric vehicle production. Earth Saviors is what they called themselves, but the name that stuck was Eco-Thugs, coined by the then governor of California, Jesus Garcia.

Over time electric cars were parked, electric airplanes were grounded, and internal combustion engine production ramped back up. Besides small ICEs that powered personal vehicles, there was a need for mammoth industrial diesel generators to keep the government running as well as hospitals, schools, and businesses. The electric grid had become unreliable. While the Eco-Thugs had a significant impact, the main problem was seemingly non-stop weather events that caused most of the power outages. Hurricanes, tornadoes, floods—all kept coming like catalogs at Christmas. The federal government instituted a crash program to get the utilities underground within a 5-year time span. The program was unfinished by the tenth year and had gone 500% over initial cost estimates. The strain on the federal budget was enormous since the utility effort coincided with efforts to relocate coastal cities to higher ground as sea levels rose.

Ten years into the Eco-Thug assaults, Jesus Garcia was elected president of the United States and soon thereafter the capitol was hit with a dirty bomb. Twenty-seven different radical groups from around the world claimed responsibility. The Eco-Thugs weren't among them, which made many feel that they were responsible. The perpetrators were never found or brought to justice. President elect Garcia was in California at the time and so escaped injury and exposure. The outgoing president declared martial law, then died of radiation induced cancer the following year.

Unknown to most Americans there were many underground facilities around the country that had been built in case of such an event. Garcia was sworn in under the wheat fields of Kansas. His first act as POTUS was issuing a presidential order declaring a million-dollar bounty on Eco-Thugs — dead or alive. Infrastructure attacks soon became few and far between.

Sean Duncan, because of his activity in the farm resistance, bumped into a few Eco-Thugs on occasion but never was a member. But some in the government believed he may have been involved.

CHAPTER 4

OBESITY COURT

The Southeast Michigan Bureau of Farm Affairs was in a large building south of Pontiac on Telegraph Road. It used to be a Mega-mart. Mega-mart, one of the country's largest employers, went out of business when 75% of their workforce left for the Farms within one year of the Grand Openings. The exodus helped get the new program off to a quick start.

Sean got the feeling back in his limbs as the Obesity Police vehicle pulled into the parking lot. The driver got out and opened the back door.

"Can you walk Mr. Duncan?"

"I think so. Give me a second to get to my feet."

The policeman helped Sean out of the car and waited while Sean tested his balance. "Where am I?' Sean asked.

"At the Obesity courthouse, Bureau of Farm Affairs."

"What happens here?"

"You'll be tested for obesity. If found guilty and your taxes are in arrears, you'll be sent to a Farm Jail to pay your debt to society."

Although a little wobbly he was able to walk in unassisted. They were met at the door by a man in a white lab coat. The police and Sean were led through a maze of cubicles each containing a lean bureaucrat. They stopped in front of a door with a sign that said "Insta-Judge". The policeman opened the door and motioned with a head jerk for Sean to enter. No one could enter the room without first stepping through a metal arch which measured height and weight instantly. Sean's BMI was flashed on a large flat screen display in large red letters – 29.6. It changed to green and 19.7 when the policeman stepped through.

Sean hadn't been in a courtroom since the day his father was convicted of euthanizing his mother. He still couldn't believe his father was sentenced to life in prison for such a merciful act. This courtroom smelled of ammonia and lacked any oak paneling. Sean stood in front of the bench while the judge finished keying in something on his OED. He looked at Sean and smiled.

"Good afternoon, Mr. Duncan."

Sean didn't answer.

"Anyway, you know why you are here. The Insta-Judge has found you guilty of obesity and you also owe a substantial amount in back taxes. Are you able to pay today?"

"I wouldn't pay even if I could. I object on moral and ethical grounds. This is lunacy."

"It is the law of the land Mr. Duncan. I sentence you to Work-Til-Twenty or 50 pounds. Your choice. You'll be going to the Jail building of the Central Iowa Farm. You don't have to decide which punishment until you check in. Enjoy your stay tonight. The bus leaves early."

"Where's Eden?" Sean asked.

"Who?"

"Eden Sprayberry. The Rexic that lied so well."

"Not everything was a lie. Her parents, Ruth and Edward, are at Central Iowa. She's in the process of earning enough money to buy ... to secure their future away from the Farms." The judge motioned to the policeman. "Please see Mr. Duncan to his holding cell."

Sean spent a restless night on an uncomfortable cot. He'd risen at 4:30 a.m. At 6 a.m. he was escorted to a minibus that left for Iowa at 6:30. Sean was the first on, and he moved to the back row. Eight men, all larger than Sean, followed him in and plopped down on the stained, oversized seats. The driver and a guard entered last. The guard turned to the group. "The trip will take about 12 hours. We will be stopping every three hours at a U.S. Burger for a bathroom break and food. You can have as many Patriot Meals as you want. We will be showing movies throughout the trip. Anyone causing any trouble will be put to sleep for the duration." The guard sat down, and the three-cylinder engine cranked, coughed, and came to life. The greasy smell of biodiesel exhaust blew in through the reinforced metal window screens.

The video monitor in front of Sean lit up. The day's entertainment started with a commercial for U.S. Burger followed by a documentary extolling the contribution of the Farms to American society. Sean watched the introduction and marveled at the numbers.

The Central Iowa Farm covered 1000 square miles, 640,000 acres. It was one of 37 such farms scattered across the United States: some larger, some smaller; all growing corn, soybeans, beef, cattle, pigs, and other food, then converting it to high grade biodiesel fuel by liposuctioning a fat human body and some simple additional steps.

Most of the two million people who lived shared a 50 square mile city. Ninety percent of them did nothing but eat and drink in front of their entertainment centers.

Whenever they had 50 pounds (about 12 gallons) of fat to pay, they did so. The Super Patriots gave 100 pounds or more per year. The minimum was 50 pounds per year before certain penalties were imposed.

Sean shook his head at the numbers and when the propaganda got too heavy, he leaned his head back and closed his eyes. He was headed for the last place on earth he wanted to be. He was unable to imagine his immediate future, but he knew he could get through it. At least he would come away with inside knowledge; perhaps something useful for the resistance. *Would his father be upset or proud?* Eden Sprayberry kept returning to his thoughts. He smiled at his own foolishness. This trip was supposed to be an adventure with her. Yesterday, in the bar, he imagined the two of them heading west, stopping somewhere in Illinois for lunch and sex. Eden was cool and lied well. Maybe she was desperate. She was so pretty. He wasn't angry, just disappointed. He worked on what he would say to her when he found her.

They stopped in Kalamazoo for the first break. The men were allowed in one at a time accompanied by the guard while the driver kept the bus idling and the door locked. When at last the guard motioned to Sean he shook his head. The guard shrugged and the bus pulled away. The thought of eating a half pound burger with bacon, double cheese and mayo along with a half pound of fries washed down with 32 ounces of triple sugar cola didn't appeal to him. The Patriot meal was at odds with his concept of patriotism. All the others brought in the red, white and blue bags; some brought in two. The smell of the French fries made Sean's stomach growl, but he knew was just getting a head start on making a 20 BMI. Still, he didn't enjoy the thought of nine more hours and two more food stops stuck in the bus with a gang of smelly Obies. He got up and stepped next to the man one seat up.

"Gonna eat all that, you fat ass?" Sean smacked the man's florid cheek with the back of his hand.

The sleep dart hit him in the chest, and he had just enough time to backpedal to his seat.

CHAPTER 5

OBESITY FARM

Sean awoke without opening his eyes. Hours of mouth breathing had left his tongue dry and swollen. He rubbed the back of his hand over the dried spittle on his cheek and then over the spot where the sleep dart hit. He lay still, listening to sounds he didn't recognize. He sensed the room was lighted and put his hand over his eyes before he opened them. He turned his head and looked at his left arm, which he hadn't been able to move. It was taped to his bed rail and connected to an IV.

"Mr. Duncan. You're awake. Welcome to Central Iowa Farm. My name is Jan."

Sean turned and looked at the nurse. She was young, plump, and smiling.

"I'll bet you're hungry and thirsty. Can I get you something?"

"Just some water, please." Sean tried to sit up. "Why am I on an IV?"

"We call it the hangover cure. The sleep darts are calibrated for a 350-pound man. For a person half that size the downtime is a lot longer and the after effects aren't too pleasant. The meds get you back to normal sooner." She set the water pitcher and glass on the nightstand and raised the head of the bed. "How do you feel?"

"Not too bad." Sean emptied the water glass and Jan refilled it. "How long have I been out?"

"The bus arrived yesterday afternoon. It's 10 AM. You're due at check-in at noon so you have time to eat and rest a little more." She walked around the bed and began removing the IV. "Let's get this off so you can get comfortable. What would you like to eat?"

"A beer and a burger."

"What brand and how do you want it cooked?"

"You're kidding."

"No sir. The Farm is all about comfort. I recommend you stick to one beer before you check in, but after that you can have all you want. All the Farms have their own breweries, distilleries, and wineries. A nice perk." Jan went to the lone desk in the room and keyed something into the terminal. "It'll be up in ten minutes. Through the door in the corner is a shower, and there's a clean jumpsuit there too."

Sean lay back and imagined a couple hundred thousand people getting blitzed daily, never leaving their apartments unless it was to get their fat sucked out, and then starting the whole process again. "Alcoholism a problem?"

Jan spun in her chair. "Not a problem exactly. The ones that overdo it can't cause any trouble, and they typically die young. It's a personal choice."

"Graveyards getting full yet?"

"There are no cemeteries. All deceased, unless picked up by a relative, become part of the energy stream."

Energy stream? Recycling the human body for its BTU content — nothing's wasted. Perhaps the muscle and organs were used for pig food and the bones for fertilizer, once stripped of all fat of course. Sean was losing his appetite. *Did Eden know all this? Why didn't Sean know? Why wasn't it common knowledge? Where was the outrage?*

Sean shook his head. "Are you supposed to be telling me all this?"

"Why wouldn't I? You're here now."

"I'll be leaving in a month or so."

"Why in the world would you want to leave?"

Sean showered and donned the green jumpsuit. It was a good fit. When he stepped out of the bathroom his food was waiting. The beer was excellent; cold and full bodied, much like a German brew. The cheeseburger was cooked perfectly and tasted delicious. Sean wished he had ordered two. The nurse had left and said someone would be by for him at noon. He found the remote and turned on the television. The Farm Channel was the only one he could get.

The Director of Central Iowa Farm was giving the past month's production numbers. His name was Sam Hawley and he smiled as he talked. Sam said that July had been another record-breaking month. The good citizens of Central Iowa had donated three million gallons of fat, and, by virtue of not needing personal vehicles, had saved an estimated 70 million gallons of fuel. The population swelled by 5281 people: 3189 births, 7242 "immigrants" and 5150 deaths.

Sean turned the program off and walked around the windowless room. The computer screen was dark, and the door locked. He rubbed a sore spot on his buttock. *Dammit! They put a tracking chip in my ass.* Had he given it any thought he would have guessed, and if he had a razor and a mirror, he would have tried to cut it out then and there. A felony no doubt.

At noon, two large men, dressed in navy blue jump-suits, came for him. They led him down a well-lit corridor, lined with identical gray doors, then out across a courtyard. Sean smelled the sweet alyssum that formed a border between the sidewalks and the perfect lawn. A half dozen dwarf apple trees held ripening fruit in the late August sun. They passed a fountain that blew a jet of water twenty feet into the air. Then they entered a brown brick building whose double doors swung open under a sign that said, "Welcome Center."

The two men handed Sean over to another plump, smiling young lady who led him through the large atrium. "You must be important," she said. "The Director himself is welcoming you." She opened a large oak door and Sean walked in.

Sean recognized Sam Hawley from the Farm Channel. Sam sat at the head of an oval conference table. Sean's escort followed him in and laid a speech-pad in front of the Director. "Mr. Duncan, sir." She turned, smiled at Sean, and left. Sam arose and shook Sean's hand. "I'm Sam Hawley. Please have a seat."

Sean sat opposite Sam. He looked around. The book-lined walls and soft lighting reminded him of his father's Washington office. Law books lined those walls of course. Here was a mixture of fiction and non-fiction from the last century. Sean wondered who read them.

"Mr. Duncan, we are honored to have the son of Senator Duncan as a guest. Your father would have been proud of your fighting spirit." Sam Hawley leaned back. "The senator...your father... fought hard. To some he's a hero. To most he just wasted his time."

"Not a waste when it's something you believe in."

"Sentimental claptrap."

"Not hardly. There's still a lot of us who believe that growing humans for fuel is disgusting and immoral."

"Certainly not the millions of patriots on the Farms." Hawley paused and looked Sean in the eye. "By the way, I'm sorry about your mother."

Sean fought the urge to leap across the table and punch Hawley in the face.

It was shortly after his father lost his second presidential election that his mother was diagnosed with bone cancer. It progressed rapidly as did the associated pain. Sean had overheard his mom saying she didn't want to go on and have her husband and son witness her deterioration. She begged for relief.

The discussions grew more frequent and intense. The National Euthanasia Law hadn't been passed at that time. Senator Duncan loved his wife dearly and was loath to consider such an act. But as the disease progressed his attitude did too. Her doctors had given Laura Duncan six to nine months. The senator lasted three before he couldn't watch her suffer any longer. He enlisted his sister Jessie, a registered nurse, to provide the required drugs and instructions. Some potassium chloride added to her IV put her quietly out of this life into a place free of pain.

"Leave it alone," Sean said.

"The senator was a few years early with that deal."

Sean evened his voice and spoke low. "My father loved my mother as much as any man loved a woman. What he did was merciful and right."

"Broke the law. Went to jail. Like father, like son."

"Kiss my ass."

"No thanks. But we can assign you to the LGBT Jail if you'd like." Sean just stared. "Bad joke. Sorry, but seriously,

I'm prepared to make you an offer. In exchange for your endorsement of the Farm System and the New American Health Act the government will cancel all your tax debt and allow you to leave after one suction. Of course you're welcome to stay as a regular Farm citizen, as I'm sure you're aware. Alternatively, you can serve your sentence and pay your back taxes."

"I want this chip out of my ass."

"Not until you leave. And if the Safe Citizen Act passes it won't come out at all."

"What would my endorsement do? The resistance is nothing, really. A bunch of derelicts for the most part, living in slums. Hardly a threat to the government or the Farm system."

"We think it would make a good recruiting poster," Sam said. "Maybe help us get a better class of people moving to the Farms."

"That makes no sense," Sean said.

"We think it does. We'd like the Farm society to be more like a cross section of the rest of America."

"I don't plan on staying, so an endorsement would be meaningless."

"You have a week to think about it. Meanwhile, enjoy your stay in the minimum-security section of Farm Jail." Sam arose and opened the door. The same two men who escorted Sean earlier were waiting on the other side. "Oh, by the way, we're testing a new type of chip in you. If it's removed by someone other than a trained technician, it will release a coma inducing toxin into your bloodstream."

The ride to the Farm Jail took thirty minutes on a smooth asphalt road that cut through vast corn fields. The crop harvest was a month away and the corn was tall and blocked any view from the back seat of the police car. The wall of corn was broken by a large building every mile or so. Traffic was light and every car that passed them was of the same color and model of the one Sean was riding in. When finally they got beyond the corn fields the landscape opened up into soybean fields. And over those the great city of the Central Iowa Farm rose like Oz in the distance.

Years ago it was called Ames, but now it was Garcia, named for the President who conceived of the Farm System as a natural adjunct to the New American Health Act. The former president spent the last years of his life here in a penthouse above the President Garcia Library. His tomb is in the center of the library grounds. From rumors, he understood the president required a double size coffin. His only memory of the president was from his childhood, sitting with his mother watching his father debate Garcia during his father's unsuccessful attempt to unseat the incumbent.

The car stopped in front of a long, low building that looked much like the Welcome Center. Same brick, smaller windows. "This is it," the driver said and unlocked the doors. "Just go in the lobby. You'll be directed to your room."

As soon as Sean got out the small car sped away. He stood in the driveway and looked for some indications that this was a jail. There were none. A half dozen men and women in green jumpsuits worked on the landscaping, pulling weeds, and trimming bushes. A couple of them waved and smiled at him. Sean had the thought to just start walking, but he had no idea of which direction, and he knew the device in his butt had to come out before any escape was possible.

Sean took another look around, then entered the building.

CHAPTER 6

BAXTER BODECKER

The lobby was empty save for a large electronic display on the facing wall. Corridors led off to the right and left. The screen lit up as he entered, and a message appeared. "Welcome Mr. Duncan. Please walk down the hallway to your right. Your room is ready." That was it. He was curious and walked into the left hall. A chime sounded and a gentle voice let him know that right was the other way.

The hallway was wide, and well lit. Numbered doors lined both sides. It reminded Sean of his grade school. About halfway down the long, empty hall a door opened as Sean approached, and the light above it began to blink. *Was the chip in his butt activating things? The lobby sign? The door lock and lamp? Yes*, thought Sean. *It's the master in my ass: my Ass Master.* Sean shook his head and went in.

It was a small apartment, certainly not a jail cell. The entry led into a living room complete with an entertainment center, sofa, and oversized recliner. On a small desk was a closed laptop computer. The carpet was plush and looked new. The entire place was spotless. An efficiency kitchen and dining area was on the left. A small hallway led to a bedroom and bathroom. Sean looked in the closets and bureau. They were stocked with additional jumpsuits, socks, underwear, and sturdy shoes. They were his size. There was even a robe and slippers.

Fresh food and beer filled the refrigerator, and a wine-rack held a full complement of reds and whites. Sean found boxes and bags of snack food in the pantry. His stomach growled. He rooted around for something that looked healthy and found a jar of peanuts. He retrieved a beer and walked to the window in the living room. Out past the building grounds hot asphalt shimmered under the thin permaclouds. Acres of soybeans stretched to the horizon, undulating in the breeze.

As he stood looking out onto the landscape, something was bothering him, and he wasn't sure what. He had been through a lot in the last few days. His entire situation was bothersome, of course, but something recent had jarred his subconscious. Sean thought back over the events of the day.

What was it that seemed out of place?

Nothing about the Farm surprised him. It upset him, yes, but surprised him, no. Except...the library where he had met the Director. It didn't fit. But there was something else, too. The smell of that conference room, the book titles. Sean was sure he had been in that room a long time ago. The only thing that came to mind was his father's library...not the one in his office, but in the house Sean grew up in. He didn't know what became of it after the government seized his father's assets. It was nasty business then, and Sean ran away from it, not having the will or the resources to fight. It was a crazy idea, but Sean had to get back to that room and open a book, see whose name might be written on the inside cover.

"Can I come in?"

Sean jumped and turned to the door he had left open. A young Black man with a round, smiling face and a 1970s afro stood in the doorway. He was holding a can of beer and was definitely an Obie. "I'm Baxter Bodecker. Didn't mean to startle you. Just get in?"

Sean waved him in and shook his hand. "I'm Sean Duncan. Pleased to meet you. Yeah, just got here." Sean sat down and motioned for Baxter to do the same. "Been here long?"

Baxter eased his bulk into an oversized armchair. "Six months next week. Tax evasion of course. You're not too fat. What did they get you for?"

"Same thing. I'm on the edge and I refuse to pay the obscene tax. I'm part of the so-called resistance." Sean got up and retrieved two more beers. He handed one to Baxter. "So, tell me about this place. It hardly seems like a jail."

"Not a jail, but certainly a prison. I've gained 30 pounds since I've been here. I'm due for my first harvesting next week. Pretty scary, but it's my own damn fault. Anyway, for someone who likes to eat and drink this is the place to be."

"Any chance to escape? Assuming one wanted to?"

"They heard that you know. But it doesn't matter. The Butt Bug will lead them to you," Baxter said. "Because of my technical background they assigned me to the Tracking Lab, working the afternoon shift. I haven't seen anyone get a quarter mile from where they're supposed to be before the guards swoop in."

Sean lowered his voice. "Do you know how to take the chip out? I was told if it wasn't removed by a trained tech I'd go into a coma."

"Really? That's a new one on me. Maybe just bullshit. But I don't know how anyway. There is a..." Baxter hesitated and looked around the room. "What say we go for a walk? Get a little fresh air."

Baxter led the way out to the rear of the jail building. "We can talk out here."

"Are all the rooms bugged?" Sean asked.

"The TVs in all the rooms have cameras and microphones that are always on. Each TV has a URL. Somewhere there's a directory of web addresses for every apartment on the Farm. So, if someone gets on your apartment page, they get a live webcam showing who's watching. Of course, if the sound is on the microphone picks up the TV too. There are SPYES in the public areas. The butt chips don't do audio, just GPS, down to a meter accuracy. One would need a Faraday shield to block the signal."

"A what?"

"A conductive shield to block the signal."

"What's a SPEYE?" Sean asked.

"Pretty much what it sounds like. Cameras watching everyone's every move."

Sean and Baxter walked around a cinder track behind the jail building. The track circled an empty soccer field. The recreation complex was large and included a softball diamond, tennis courts, and horseshoe pits. The only other people there were tending the grounds. No one was exercising.

"So you're saying that I can wear tin foil shorts and defeat the tracking chip?"

Baxter chuckled. "No. All I meant was that wrapping some aluminum foil around your middle can reduce the signal strength to some extent. You'd have to be shielded head to foot to really do the job. An electrically conductive set of clothes would be the ticket, but running around in tin foil would be uncomfortable I'm thinking."

"Is there such a thing as conductive paint?" Sean asked.

"Yes there is, but I doubt you'll find any at Farm Jail."

Baxter pulled a handkerchief out of his back pocket and wiped the sweat off his forehead. "Why do you want to get out so bad? You might want to give it a chance just to see if you like it here."

Sean ignored Baxter's question and looked over the sports complex. "Where is everybody? Why aren't people out here playing games or exercising?"

"I think they planned for a larger jail population. We're only about a quarter full. Most everyone opts to become a law-abiding member of the Farm. Seems the pleasures of the flesh are too great a temptation for a lot of people. When I came in, I was convinced I'd do my time and pay my fat then get the hell out. But man, it's getting tougher to convince myself I'm gonna leave."

"Don't do it. The Farms are an abomination. I'm getting out one way or another. If you want, I'll take you with me. Together we can figure a way out. You said you were scared to go for your first harvest? Well don't." Sean hoped his sense that Baxter wasn't a spy was correct. "You got family outside?"

"A skinny sister that agrees with you about the Farms. She visited me a month ago. Swore she'd never come back."

"Well, think of her when you contemplate wasting your life in here."

Baxter sat down on a park bench. His overalls were half wet with sweat. "I gotta go to work. Working afternoons this week. I'll see what I can find out about that coma thing. If it's bullshit, we can cut each other's chip out if we decide it's the best thing to do. They aren't too deep. I can't believe I'm saying this. Must be I need some excitement. Did you open your Cackle account?"

"What's that?"

"It's what passes for social media on the Farms. You can

use the laptop in your room. Get on the Farm Web and search for Cackle. It's fairly useless unless you want to make a lot of fat friends who jabber about what's on TV and in the refrigerator."

"They should have named it Oink."

By five that afternoon, Sean was sitting in his apartment sipping a glass of Merlot, wondering if had said too much to Baxter. He didn't think so; he'd always been a pretty good judge of character. Baxter was open, funny, and friendly.

Then there was Eden Sprayberry. Maybe he wasn't such a good judge where pretty women are concerned. He wasn't mad at her, a little angry at himself for sure, but he understood her motivation. If his parents were here, he'd have done the same. It was too late to worry about it now. Now he just wanted to formulate a plan to escape this madness. But not before finding out how his father's personal library might have ended up in a building at the Central Iowa Farm. He went to the small desk with the laptop and opened a Cackle account.

CHAPTER 7

ESCAPE

Sean slept well despite his foreign surroundings, due in no small part to the relaxing properties of the Merlot. He felt good after his shower. The digital scale in the bathroom told him he had only gained a half pound in the past week, an amount within the margin of error of the scales. The clothes closet held a rack of jump suits in ascending sizes, anticipating his weight gain. That gave him an idea for an experiment. He'd need Baxter's help to see if his idea worked. He would also need a roll of aluminum foil and some duct tape. He found a roll of foil in the kitchen, but there wasn't tape of any kind in the apartment. Sean pulled on a clean jumpsuit and went for a walk.

It was still early, and the hall was empty save for a large woman pushing a maid's cart. A Labrador retriever followed the woman, sitting when she stopped. Sean approached her. "Good morning. How are you?"

"I'm just fine, young man. And you?" Her gray hair was pulled up in a bun and she moved with some difficulty. Her jumpsuit was bright yellow with the word "MAINTENANCE" in black across her stooped back.

"I'm okay." Sean bent over and petted the dog. "What's your dog's name?"

"Rollo. Keeps me company. He's not mine. He's the building's mascot."

"I was just wondering where I might find some tape to hold my old bible together. I broke the binding last night." It was the only reason Sean could come up with for needing the tape.

"There might be some in the storeroom. Follow me."

Sean followed her and Rollo down the hall and into a room the size of his apartment. He walked slowly among the racks of toilet paper, detergent, and plastic trash bags. He noted the mops and buckets, looking for anything that may be of some use for someone on the run. In one corner a leather tool belt hung from a peg. A roll of duct tape hung from the belt. He stuffed the tape into his overalls and thought about taking the hammer too but decided against it.

"Find any tape?" the maid asked when Sean came out.

"No. That's okay. I'll just have to be careful reading it."

"I didn't think anyone read the bible anymore."

Sean returned to his apartment, locked the door, and went into the bedroom, out of the range of the television. He got out another jump suit of the size he was wearing and one the next size up. He smiled at the thinking behind a larger size suit. They know most people need them after a month or so on the farm diet. He laid the smaller one on the bed and started wrapping it in aluminum foil. When he finished a leg, he wrapped the foil in duct tape. He continued until the entire suit was covered. With a steak knife he sliced the metal cover open along the suit's long front zipper. Then he unzipped the larger suit and slid the foil cover suit into it. It was heavy and wouldn't be the easiest thing to run around in. If he tried it on now and it did kill the homing signal it would alert the guards. No, he'd have to wait for Baxter to help him test it.

Sean spent the day watching television, eating, and drinking. That night he slept the sleep of someone who was mentally and physically exhausted with a bottle of Merlot in his system.

He awoke at seven and felt a little groggy, but decent. He showered, got dressed and made himself some bacon and eggs. Baxter knocked at eight.

"Good morning, Sean."

"Good morning, Baxter. Anything new?"

Baxter turned up the volume on the TV then whispered, "Let's talk in the bathroom. No CAM in there."

Sean sat on the toilet lid and Baxter sat on the edge of the bathtub.

"The coma business is bogus as far as I can tell. I've made a few friends in the lab that seem to be straight shooters. No one had heard of a new chip being introduced. They'd be the first to know." Baxter burped and took another swig from his can of Capitol Cola. "So, I guess we could cut them out. If you left it in your bedroom at bedtime, you'd have about eight hours to get somewhere. After that they'd send someone over to see why you're not moving."

"And if your signal disappears?" Sean asked.

"Here in a flash to inject a new one in the other cheek. Then they'll schedule an appointment to remove the old one and do a failure analysis. I've only seen one failure in the time I've been here."

"I guess my Tin Man suit isn't such a good idea." Sean went into the bedroom and retrieved his aluminum lined jumpsuit. "What do you think?"

Baxter spewed cola on his ample stomach. "Ha! I love that, man. Have you tried it on? No. You couldn't have. But it might be fun to see how long before the dogs found you."

"Dogs. Didn't even think of that. The eight-hour head start sounds like a better idea. We'll need to cut the Butt Bugs out. Any chance of stealing a car?"

"You're serious, aren't you?" Baxter got to his feet and took the suit from Sean. He held it up and admired it before laying it over the sink. "If I can get a car, will you take me with you?"

Sean smiled. "I said I would. I'll need your help finding my way out. What's it going to take?"

"The lab has several cars in their carpool. They don't need keys. They let me use one every other Friday to pick up supplies and Chinese. Pieces of shit, but they always run. We'd need to have our bugs out, but in our pockets, and we'll need to be on the same sleep schedule. I should be off the afternoon shift in a couple of weeks."

Sean frowned. "Two weeks?"

"It'll give us time to make a plan. We need a plan," Baxter said.

"You're right. It'll give me some time to learn a little more about this place." Sean picked up the foil lined suit. "The best way to learn about the enemy is to see them in action."

"You're not..."

"Why not? I want to see the director again anyway. I'll be back." Sean slipped into the bulky suit, left his apartment, and hustled down the hallway through the doors, out into the humid afternoon.

CHAPTER 8

TRACKING LAB

The Tracking Laboratory was in a low, gray building several miles from the Farm Jail. It was on a cleared corner of a large soybean field. A tall cell tower stood nearby. There were no signs to identify it. The lab vehicles were also unmarked save for a number on the rear bumper. The few windows were all tinted. A trained eye could spot the CCTV cams along the eaves. Inside, the main section was filled with work benches with monitors and electronic repair tools, supplies, and old desks with monitors glowing in the dimmed LED overhead lighting.

Baxter sat at his bench, three large monitors in front of him. One monitor was a spreadsheet of the live tracking devices currently in use. The cells were green unless a transmitter went dead or left its assigned zone. Then it turned red, and an alarm sounded. The second monitor was connected to the Farm Wide Web. Baxter got on the lab's website and clicked on the Technical Manuals hyperlink. He opened the latest manual on the tracking system. He had never bothered to read the theory of operation before, having no need. It was obvious to him what it was for and how it worked. Today he hoped to dig a little deeper to determine if there was a newer version that could induce a coma upon unauthorized removal. He found no such thing mentioned in the manual.

Baxter was also tasked with repairing electronics in the Tracking Lab's carpool. Radios, alternators, ABS and GPS systems—he enjoyed the work. Electronics were the most reliable thing on the vehicles. He hadn't had to repair a radio or GPS system. The third monitor on his lab bench displayed a spreadsheet showing the locations of every vehicle in the pool. Clicking on the cell pulled up a report on the vehicle's condition. Baxter cycled through the half dozen or so vehicles noting that there were no major issues. A few were due for oil changes.

Baxter shared the late shift with a co-worker named Xavier. He was an Obie and hailed from Cleveland, Ohio. He had worked at the lab for several years and enjoyed the Farm's easy life. He contributed often to the Fat Man and his scars showed it. They got along well.

"Xavier! You got anything going?"

"Nah, man. Things are quiet as usual. But that's alright. Don't need any surprises this evening."

"We never get any surprises. Some surprises might be fun. What are you doing tonight?"

"Not a damn thing," Xavier replied.

"Me neither. I'm going to take a break. Can you handle all this work?" Baxter laughed.

"Not an issue. I got it covered. Wake me when you get back."

Baxter walked out to the parking lot and looked around. It was insanely quiet in the bean field. The parking lot lamps cast a dim light and were swarming with moths. The Tracking Lab vehicles were collecting dust. He walked up to one and opened the door. The inside was clean. He closed the door and stepped back to view the roof. The GPS antenna was on the passenger side front corner. Baxter looked around before he reached up, grabbed the antenna, and snapped it off. He opened the door and threw it in the back seat. He took note of the vehicle number before returning to the lab.

"That was quick," Xavier said.

"Yeah. Just needed to stretch my legs." Baxter sat down on his lab stool and called up the status of the vehicle he had visited. It showed a broken GPS and a full tank of biodiesel.

CHAPTER 9

CORN DOG

Sean jogged toward the nearest cornfield, which was just beyond the recreation area. The rows ran perpendicular to his direction, ending at a road a quarter mile to his left, and stretching as far as he could see to his right. He plunged in, fighting his way twenty rows deep. The aluminum trapped his body heat. Sweat burned his eyes and soaked the inside of his triple-layer suit. He stopped to catch his breath and unzipped down to his waist to let some body heat escape. He left the zipper down, turned to the right, and began walking between the drying stalks. Every few minutes he crossed a row, getting deeper into the corn. The corn was a good two feet taller than Sean, and it shielded him from being seen from above. He expected to hear a helicopter or see a drone at any moment, but there was only the rustling of the leaves as he walked down the narrow lane.

He knew he risked being moved to a higher security prison after he was caught, but he thought he could talk his way into a second chance if he showed any signs of a willingness to vouch for the Farms. There was a chance, of course, that he wouldn't see Director Hawley after this. The director might interpret it as his final answer. Sean suspected that Hawley would want to see the suit he had fashioned. Maybe he'd even put it in the Farm Historical Museum.

He had walked for perhaps twenty minutes and still hadn't reached the end of the cornfield. Sweat ran in rivulets down his back. He pulled an ear of corn from a stalk, and peeled it, hoping that the kernels held enough moisture to quell his burgeoning thirst. They were hard and bitter. He spat them out and continued walking. When finally he could see the edge of the corn, he stopped to consider his next move.

Whether he heard something, or simply sensed it, he wasn't sure, but he turned slowly to look at his back track. An eighty-pound, black German shepherd sat five yards behind him, yellow eyes locked to his, tongue lolling out of its panting mouth. The dog simply kept its distance as Sean walked backwards out to the road where Sam Hawley himself was waiting in the back seat of the idling security wagon.

"That was a dumb stunt, Mr. Duncan, although I do admire your creative tailoring skills. Your week is almost up. I'll send someone to pick you up in the morning so that we can discuss the remainder of your stay."

The wagon sat idling in the parking lot of the minimum-security facility. The driver sat silently petting the shepherd on the seat next to him. "That's it? I can just go back to my room?" Sean said.

"You look like you could use a shower and a cold drink. I'm confident you'll throw your new suit in the trash. Of course, if you decide to wear it again we'll likely send out a less friendly dog. See you in the morning."

Baxter was waiting in Sean's room, and handed him a

cold beer when he walked in. "Took them about 90 minutes. Not bad."

Sean stripped to his underwear and dropped the sodden suit on the floor. He drank two glasses of ice water before cracking the beer. "How did they know where I was going to pop out of the corn?" Sean asked. "Duh, the dog was bugged," answering his own question. "Which reminds me. The cleaning lady had an old Lab following her around. Can people have pets here?"

"Sure. Not too many people would agree to move here if they had to leave Rover at home," Baxter said. "There's plenty of wildlife running around too. Deer, turkey, stray cats."

"Any more thoughts on the car?"

"I picked a car on my last shift and disabled the GPS. It has a full tank of gas. We should have enough time to drive to the city and ditch it. Once we're in the city we might be able to hide long enough to figure out how to make it past the border. No way we can drive out. Maybe hop a freight train if there are any still running."

Sean smiled. The border – an imaginary line separating the farms from the old USA. *We are in a foreign country,* he thought. What would his father have made of all this? "I'm seeing the Director in the morning. I think I can buy myself another week here. If so, let's plan on next Friday. If not, I'm not sure what I'm going to do."

Baxter took a swig of beer. "You'll be back," he said.

The next morning the security vehicle arrived at 8:30 to pick Sean up. By then he had showered, dressed, and eaten a light breakfast of coffee and peanut butter toast. Neither the driver nor Sean said a word on the way to the Welcome Center.

"You know the way," the driver said as he stopped in at the front entrance. Sean got out and made his way to the conference room.

"Have you given any thought to what we discussed earlier this week?" Director Hawley didn't look up from his computer until he closed the lid. Then he smiled at Sean. "You're looking quite well today. Yesterday's exercise must have agreed with you."

"I really didn't think I'd get very far. Just horsing around. Boredom." Sean feigned a sheepish smile. "I'd like another week to think it over. I must say, the accommodations are quite good. You guys don't make it easy."

"I can give you another week, but you'll need to start contributing to the Farm."

"I've gained a pound since I came in," Sean said.

"That's a start. Keep in mind we're just asking for an endorsement. I believe that if Senator Duncan could see all the good that the Farms do for the country, he himself would endorse them."

"I doubt it," Sean said, getting up from his chair. "Can I borrow a couple of these books?" He scanned the shelves. "It'll help with the boredom. Have you read any of these?"

"I don't read books. No one reads books. These were here when I arrived. Help yourself."

Sean took some time studying the titles. He finally selected Zinn's *A People's History of the United States*, and Clark's *Against All Enemies: Inside America's War on Terror*. "I appreciate it. I'll bring them back when I'm finished."

"Don't bother."

"Thanks."

Sean was sent back to his building via robocab. He held the books in his lap without opening them and wondered what he would find inside the front covers. *Funny how some things stick in the mind*, he thought as a clear memory arose — it was of his father signing his name on the inside front cover of books he'd brought home or received in the mail. Then he'd follow his own system of shelving the titles or leaving books to be read on a small table next to his favorite red velvet and mahogany chair.

The family library was his favorite room in the house. A remembered smell of paper, ink, fabric, glue, and dust rushed into his head. In his mind's eye, he saw winter's light streaming through the windows, past the heavy brocade drapes tied back with tassels and attached to the dark wood frames. It always felt warmer in the library than in any other room. In summers, when the windows were open to welcome cross breezes, it was a joy for Sean to sit with his back against a large pillow on the floor and read.

He had no clear memories of his father in any other room at home except in the kitchen on mornings when the Senator folded his newspaper, poured a cup of coffee into a travel mug for his commute to his Washington office, and patted Sean on the head while telling him to "learn something new today, son."

Sean closed the door to his apartment and set the books on the kitchen table. He cracked a beer and sat down. Zinn was on top. He opened the cover. There, in sprawling cursive: *Darius Oliver Duncan.*

CHAPTER 10

PAIN IN THE ASS

Sean spent the week learning all he could about the metropolis of Garcia. Of the five hundred satellite television channels available, fully one third of them were related to the Farms; their history, the cities, culture, government, and any number of poorly produced local shows.

Garcia boasted a population of two million people. Most lived in government-built apartment complexes that were more like self-contained villages. One could be born, live, and die without ever leaving the building. A few residents had done just that. Farm employees, depending on their status, could live in detached houses; six hundred square foot, energy efficient, look-alike homes with shared common outdoor spaces. There were pockets of these houses throughout Garcia. Workers were required to live within easy walking distance of their jobs.

While Sean studied Garcia's city layout, Baxter's job was to determine the best way to remove the butt bugs and to assemble the necessary things to do it. He also was responsible for showing up in a vehicle that had no GPS. They could be in downtown Garcia in thirty minutes. They would need to find some civilian clothes and make an attempt to disguise their appearance as best they could. The rest of the plan was non-existent.

Since Baxter had access to the Farm Wide Web in his workplace. Sean asked him to find the name and addresses of anybody named Sprayberry who lived in Central Iowa. There was only one listing. Sean was thankful that Eden wasn't Eden Smith.

"Who's she?" Baxter asked.

"She's the reason I am where I am today. I'll explain on the way to the city."

Along with the address, Baxter printed out a map to the building. If they had to hide out it might as well be in a place where Sean had a chance to meet someone he knew.

Baxter showed up at 10 p.m. on Friday night. "Let's do this in the john. No SPEYES. I have forty-five minutes before they expect me back," he said. "I asked my boss if I could go home for dinner. He didn't give a shit. Nice guy, but dumb. Let's get these bugs out." He dumped the contents of a plastic bag on the bathroom counter. There was a bottle of alcohol, single edge razor blades, butterfly bandages, cotton balls, and tweezers. "You're first," Baxter said.

Sean looked at the items. "Be gentle." He pulled down his jump suit and bent over the counter. Baxter found the fresh mark where the chip was inserted and swabbed it with alcohol. He made a small incision and pushed the tweezers in. "Shit, that hurts," Sean said.

"Got it!" Baxter dropped the bloody device on the counter. "Hang on while I slap on a bandage."

"Ouch. Easy big guy," Sean said. He wiped up the blood with a paper towel and pulled up his clothes. "Your turn."

"You're going to have a harder time. I've got a lot of fat to dig through. It's right here." Baxter put his finger where he knew the chip had been inserted. "Don't worry about hurting me. No pain. No gain."

It took two minutes, but Sean finally dug out the chip. "Sorry man. You okay?"

Baxter stood up. "Yeah. I'm okay." His face was sweaty. "Don't mix them up. Put yours in your bedroom. Not sure what I'm going to do with mine."

"I've got that covered. Rinse off your chip and put it in your pocket. Grab your go bag. I'll meet you in the lobby." Sean threw his chip on his bed and grabbed the bag he had packed. He stopped to grab a slice of American cheese from the refrigerator then went to meet Baxter. In the lobby Sean waved the cheese under the sleeping Rollo's nose and got him to follow them into the car. "Give me your chip." Baxter did, and Sean rolled it up in the cheese. Rollo swallowed it in one bite. "Ready?"

Baxter reached up and tore out the flimsy roof liner. He ripped out some wires from the electronics that were now exposed. "That was the radio transmitter. I'm ready now."

Ten minutes later they stopped and let Rollo out next to thousands of acres of soybeans.

"So, tell me about Eden Sprayberry," Baxter said. They were halfway to the city limits and the glow of civilization reflected off the permaclouds.

"I was hiding out in a safe house in Detroit while the Obesity Police did a sweep in my neighborhood. The place is a dump, full of derelicts, dopers, and drunks. Out of no-where this good-looking, well-dressed woman shows up and starts asking questions. Said she was looking for a guy who I happened to know. Said her folks told her to talk to him about the farms. I told her he had died, and she started to leave. I volunteered to walk her out to where she could catch a cab. We stopped for a beer and a nice chat. I hadn't been with a woman in ages, and I was falling in love. When we finally made it out of Detroit, she opened her OED and moments later the cops show up and shoot me with a sleep dart."

"Wow. So now you're going to do what exactly?"

"I don't know. Tell her I'm not mad and could she help get us out of here," Sean said. "Slow down. There should be some industrial parks up ahead."

The city of Garcia sat amid a ring of industries that supported the people and infrastructure: food processing, waste processing, recycling centers, power, water, and of course, the biodiesel refineries. The air smelled like the fry room of a U.S. Burger and vibrated with a low industrial hum. Plumes of steam rose from hundreds of rooftop stacks. No one was out walking in this part of town. Only a minimum of overhead lamps illuminated the damp streets.

Baxter pulled in behind a recycling center where huge bins held the separated discards of the city. He parked next to one that was labeled TEXTILES. They both looked around for SPYES, the ubiquitous video cams that kept watch on the citizenry. They saw only one. It was hanging by its cable, pointing down. They got out and went to the bin.

"Let's hope we get lucky." Sean opened the bin and began throwing old clothes out onto the ground. Anything that looked promising he tossed to Baxter who held up the piece to see if it would fit him. "Whoa. I think we hit the mother lode." Sean pulled out a wad of yellow jumpsuits with MAINTENANCE printed across the back. "I hope a couple of these will fit. Stained and wrinkled, but they'll work."

"The maintenance folks must be big," Baxter said. "You may have to roll up the sleeves and legs."

They picked out two of the best-looking uniforms and changed into them. "I was going to suggest ditching the car here, but with these outfits we may be safe driving a little closer to Eden's building," Sean said.

"I'm not into walking any more than I have to." Baxter slid in behind the wheel. "Let's get out of this area. It's creepy."

"Let's see if anybody's out and about," Sean said. "Turn right. I think that will get us to the main drag."

Despite being near midnight on a Friday there were a great many people walking around in downtown Garcia. The streets were busy, with many Rexics and Obies enjoying themselves. Sean watched a few Obies out for a stroll, having ventured out of one of the large apartment buildings. A minibus pulled up in front of a theater, and a group of fat, older women came out and squeezed into it. It drove two blocks and stopped in front of a Chinese restaurant. The women all got off and went inside.

"Let's find a quiet place to park," Sean said.

Baxter drove a mile past the busiest section of Corn Row—the city's main drag—pulled the car down a quiet side street and parked it. He and Sean studied the map then struck out walking. The building they wanted was a mile to the north. Away from the downtown area the streets were empty, and when the streetlamps winked out at midnight Sean and Baxter felt a little more secure.

Central Iowa Building 60 stood four stories tall and a quarter mile long. It was typical of most of the residence buildings. The ground floor was a public area visible through large windows from the street and was composed of shops, a large public area, and a rarely used exercise room. The lower two levels were basements and held the building mechanicals, food prep, laundry, suctioning rooms, and medical. All this Sean learned from the Farm television shows. The top three floors were all apartments, accessible by elevators and escalators. The narrow stairways were required by the fire code but were seldom if ever used.

"Are we just going to walk in?" Baxter asked.

"Might as well. There shouldn't be any APBs out on us yet. They think I'm sleeping and that you're roaming around the crop lands. With any luck there won't be any real maintenance people this time of night." Sean approached one of the many large glass doors. It opened automatically.

"This is pretty neat," Baxter said. "Let's go downstairs and find a place to crash. I'm pretty wiped."

The public area was softly lit, cool, and quiet. Sean and Baxter found a fire exit sign and entered the stairwell. "Let's go down and look around. See if we can find some civilian clothes somewhere," Sean said.

"And some food, and a place to sack out," Baxter said.

Sean led the way down to the first basement level. They walked past locked rooms with stenciled numbers on them, past open storerooms containing everything from toilet paper to tomato paste. Baxter went into several looking for food. He found some crackers in one and canned sardines in another. He ate them as they explored the hallways.

"There should be a laundry down here," Sean said. "There are no washers and dryers in the apartments. Everyone sends their clothes down in bags to a community laundromat. It's another energy saving thing."

"I hear it," Baxter said.

They followed the sound to the laundry room. Several dozen industrial washers and dryers were sloshing and spinning against the far wall. Two women stood at a gleaming stainless-steel table, folding clothes and stuffing them back into orange mesh bags. They spotted Sean and Baxter before the men could duck back into the hall but returned to their work without a word. Sean looked at Baxter and shrugged.

"Hello ladies. How are you?" Sean smiled.

"Hate midnights. Too much work" the older of the two women said. "You here to fix that dryer?" She cocked her head toward the row of machines, one of which was stopped.

"Yeah, we'll take a look at it," Sean said. Baxter and Sean pretended to examine the broken dryer. "Shit, there's got to be clothes here that would fit us. I wonder how long they're working?"

"I got an idea," Baxter said. He approached the steel table. "Ladies, is it almost time for your break? We're going to have to shut everything down for a half an hour while we disconnect the broken dryer."

"It's always time for a break," the younger one said. They stopped folding and left.

"Good job, Baxter." Sean went to the door and watched the women disappear down the corridor. "Gotta be quick," he said. It took ten minutes for Sean and Baxter to rummage through and find a set of clothes for each of them. They changed quickly and stuffed their yellow jumpsuits under the clothes in a bin marked DECEASED. After unplugging the stopped dryer and leaving the door open, they hurried to basement level two, to find a place to sleep.

The staircase ended in a dimly lit, narrow hallway. It was dank, and the air hummed with the sound of large machinery. "Pumps?" Sean wondered aloud.

"That's going to make for some sound sleeping," Baxter said.

"Good one Baxter. Hopefully, it'll drown out your snoring – in case you do."

There were no doors on this level; the hallway opened onto large rooms every fifty feet or so. They stuck their heads in a couple, not finding a decent spot to hide. Finally, they found one that had a forest of large pipes from floor to ceiling – some marked water, others marked waste.

"This'll work," Sean said.

CHAPTER 11

EDEN SPRAYBERRY

The fugitives lay on the floor behind a row of foot-thick water pipes.

"Good night Baxter," Sean said as he tried to get comfortable. Baxter was already snoring.

The thrum of the pipes and the men's physical weariness kept them out for hours. Sean awoke first. It took him a minute to realize where he was. He slowly stretched then nudged Baxter. "It's time to start our weekend, partner. I say we visit the Sprayberrys."

Baxter grunted and rolled over. "My ass hurts," He sat up and yawned. "I hope they have some coffee."

"I hope they let us in."

"Remind me why we're going to visit them," Baxter said.

"I'm hoping Eden is there or at least I find out where she lives. I want to know why she turned me in to the police. And, as I told you before, I was falling in love before I got zapped."

They made their way up to the commons area on the first floor and stopped in the exercise shower room to wash up and comb their hair. Their go bags contained a few essentials, but not razors. Both men had started beards, hoping for some measure of disguise. "We're looking kind of grubby already," Baxter said to Sean's reflection in the large mirror.

There were a few citizens up and about, and no one gave a second glance to Sean and Baxter. They used the elevator to get to the fourth floor where Eden's parents lived in apartment 4111.

"What are you going to say?" Baxter asked.

"I'm just going to tell them Eden told me to look them up and say hi."

"And then?"

"I'll just wing it. Chit chat about Michigan. Whatever." Sean knocked on the door.

After a slight delay the door opened a crack and Eden's face appeared. Sean jammed his foot in the door. "Don't slam it. I just came by to say hi. Honest. No hard feelings. We could use a cup of coffee."

Eden backed away and let them in. She looked to Sean like she had aged in the few short weeks since he had first met her. She was still pretty, but her eyes revealed sadness and a lack of sleep. "What are you doing here? How did you find me?"

"Eden, meet my friend Baxter. Baxter, Eden." Baxter shook her hand and closed the door. "Baxter looked your parents up on the Farm Wide Web. We thought we'd stop by to say hi. I had no idea you were here. Are you all right?"

Eden fought back tears. "No. No I'm not. Both my parents are dead." She put her hands on her face, and Sean put his arms around her and held her until she regained some composure.

"I'm sorry. What happened?"

Eden wiped her eyes and blew her nose. "My dad had a heart attack during suctioning. Mom had a heart attack when she found out."

"Wow," Baxter said. "That's...wow."

"I was going to make some smartass remark about you using me to get your folks out of here, but I guess I won't. I lost my parents when I was still young, so I do know what you're going through. I am sorry."

"Do you hate me?" Eden asked.

"No. But I wouldn't hate you a lot more if you could make us some coffee."

Eden smiled. "I'll make some. Please sit down."

Sean and Baxter sat on opposite ends of the sofa. The apartment was similar to Sean's in its layout. The Sprayberrys had decorated it with mementos and photographs of their life. Next to Sean, on the end table, was a framed photo of Eden, at about ten years old he guessed, sitting on a pony, complete with cowboy hat and boots. Her high school graduation picture hung on the wall behind Baxter. Sean looked to the television wall. It was showing a large picture of him. The pictured morphed slowly from a clean-shaven Sean to Sean with a three-day growth, then back again.

Eden came back from the kitchen and looked at the screen. "You're famous," she said.

"Busted," Baxter said.

"It's all a misunderstanding," Sean said. "They think I should stay on the Farm for a while. But I really don't want to." He looked at Eden. "You going to turn me in again?"

"No, never again. I felt terrible after that business in Detroit. I came close to not going through with it. I'm sorry."

"Not as sorry as I am. I was hoping to keep you company on the ride out here. But now maybe Baxter and I can ride home with you."

"Hey. There's me," Baxter said. "Rollo must have taken a dump."

"What?" Eden looked confused.

"I'll tell you about our great escape over breakfast," Sean said. "I'll cook."

Baxter's stomach growled audibly as the aroma of fresh coffee filled the air. Sean filled Eden in on the details of their getaway over a breakfast of eggs, bacon, pancakes, and hash browns.

Eden pushed her food around the plate. "So, what do you do now?" she asked. "I'm leaving in a couple of days. The funeral service is tomorrow. Then I'm packing up a few things here and heading back to Michigan."

"Funeral service?" Sean asked.

"The Farm has a service for all residents who request it or have a relative that does. There's a small chapel in each apartment building. My parents will be laid out tomorrow morning at ten. Then their bodies will be shipped home."

"I thought everyone got to become part of the 'energy stream'," Sean said.

"Most do. I'm lucky. Mom and father bought burial plots years ago. Otherwise I couldn't take them home."

"I'd love to attend, but I'm afraid that's out of the question."

"You can watch it on the Funeral Channel." Eden picked up the remote and switched channels. There was a service in progress. The screen was split between a close-up of an open casket and a shot of the small chapel. Two people sat in the front pew. The deceased male looked to be no older than forty. His face was round and red. It almost seemed to glow in the soft chapel light.

"He doesn't look right," Baxter said.

"He's dead, you moron." Sean laughed.

"Not when that picture was taken. I'll bet that's a holographic image based on photos taken when he was alive. Gotta be. Either that or the morticians here are magicians."

"Why would they do that?" Sean asked.

"They probably feed these to the Web. The worldwide one," Baxter said. "Relatives can attend a cyber-service and think they're seeing a real body. But the body is long gone – up in smoke as it were. Interesting."

Sean looked at Eden. "Kiss your parents' cheeks tomorrow. Just to be sure."

Eden turned off the screen and fought back tears. "I hate this fucking place."

A knock on the door brought the three to their feet. "You expecting anyone?" Sean whispered.

Eden shook her head and motioned them toward the bedroom. She stood behind the door. "Who is it?"

"Security, ma'am. May we come in?"

"I'm not dressed. What is it?"

"We have reason to believe that a couple of jail escapees may be in this building. We don't think they're dangerous, but we just want all the residents to be aware."

"I saw their pictures on TV this morning. I'll be sure to let you know if I see them."

"Have a good day, ma'am."

Eden opened the bedroom door. "That didn't take them long," Baxter said. "If they bring the dogs, we're screwed."

"Can we borrow your car?" Sean asked. "I promise we'll get it back to you before you need it."

"What if you get caught?"

"I'll tell them we forced you to give us the keys. You'll get it back one way or another."

Eden found her purse and dug out her car key. "It's the light green Honda Earth. It's in the visitor's lot. I think we can see it from the balcony."

Eden walked out on the small balcony while Sean and Baxter hung back. "It's in the last row nearest the road. It's to the left from here, second spot from the end. Eden stepped further out and look up and down the lot. She stepped back in. "There's a man in a blue jumpsuit leading a German Shepherd between the rows of cars," Eden said.

CHAPTER 12

THE PRESIDENTIAL LIBRARY

The three moved back from the sliding door and watched as the security guard finished checking the parking lot. He went out of their view as he headed toward the building.

"Time to go," Sean said. "When they show up at your door tell them you wouldn't let us in. They'll track us down to the lot." Sean handed her keys back to Eden. "We'll have to steal someone else's car." He looked at Baxter.

"Piece of cake," Baxter said.

Sean turned to Eden. "When are you leaving?"

"Tuesday morning."

"Keep your TV on. If you don't see a report of our capture, we'll be here begging for a ride."

"Where will you go?"

"The Garcia Presidential Library."

"We're going to steal a car so we can go to a library?"

Baxter looked perplexed. "I thought we were heading for the farm border."

"You can drop me off if you want, but I need to do some research. Eden, can we get a couple of bottles of water?"

"Of course, but why the library?"

Sean went into the kitchen and took two bottles of water from the refrigerator. He handed one to Baxter.

"What..."

Sean cut Eden off. "I want to see if there's any clues there that might help me find out what happened to my father."

"Your father?"

"Senator Darius Oliver Duncan. His library — the library that was in the house I grew up in—is in a room in the Welcome Center. I need to know why."

"Your father was Senator Duncan?" Eden looked at Baxter.

"I didn't know either," Baxter said.

"We have got to go." Sean put his hands on Eden's shoulders and pulled her close. She didn't resist. He kissed her on her cheek. "Thanks. I'll see you Tuesday if not sooner."

"Yeah, thanks," Baxter shrugged and followed Sean out the door and down the hall to the first stairwell.

At the ground level exit Sean cracked the door open and checked for security. The lot was empty. He and Baxter went out and walked among the cars, looking for one with a set of keys in it. Since crime was almost unheard of in the Farms it wasn't such a long shot. They didn't find one. "Let's take the security guy's car," Baxter said.

"Good thinking," Sean said.

The unlocked Farm vehicle sat empty in a far corner of the lot. Baxter ripped out the GPS assembly, and they drove out. Black storm clouds rolled in under the perma-cloud layer, threatening rain. Traffic was light, as usual, just delivery vans, buses, and a few tourists. Sean had a good mental map of where they were and where the library was located. They would need to abandon the stolen car and walk as soon as possible.

"Head south. There's an old university bell tower a mile or so north of the library, which is south of here," Sean said. "Let's park there."

Baxter headed south and spotted the bell tower after a twenty-minute drive. He pulled onto a side street near it as the rains came. They started walking. Any scent trail would wash away in the warm downpour.

They walked for half an hour, looping around one of the cookie-cutter house neighborhoods. Sean had taken the government umbrella from the stolen security car, and despite Baxter's bulk, the two managed to stay mostly dry. Now the rain moved on, and the humidity climbed with the afternoon temperature. Sean had brought a city map he had found in his apartment, he stopped to consult it. They turned toward the President Garcia Mall. "Almost there," Sean said.

The President Garcia Mall was modeled after the old Washington, D.C. Mall. At one end of the reflecting pool was the President Garcia monument. Past the other end of the pond was a quarter mile of gardens and open green space ending at the Garcia Presidential Library. The Mall had become a must-see tourist attraction in the Midwest. Peak season was April and May, when the gardens were in bloom, and before the heat of summer set in. There were few tourists this time of year.

Sean and Baxter sat at the foot of President Garcia's massive statue. The statue was a rough copy of the Lincoln monument with the main difference being that President Garcia held a glass of whiskey in one hand and a cigar in the other. Also, it was larger. Garcia was entombed in a crypt below it.

Pigeons waddled around looking for handouts. Plump golden koi rolled in the pool, sending ripples across its shining surface.

"This place is pretty cool," Baxter said. "It's not so impressive on TV. Why is his library in Iowa?"

"This was the first farm to open and he wanted this obscene monument to be part of it. President Garcia was a moron."

"Your father ran against him, didn't he?"

Sean stood up. "Yes. Twice. He tried to unseat him, but Garcia won re-election in a landslide. A lot of people liked the thought of getting free room and board for several hundred pounds of flesh. After the election my mother was diagnosed with cancer. She was suffering horribly. My father couldn't stand to see her in so much pain, so he gave her something to put her out of her misery. It wasn't legal in Maryland at the time. He was convicted of murder and sent away to prison. I went to live with my aunt in Michigan. My father wasn't in prison a year when we were notified that he had escaped. That was the last we heard of him. He was never re-captured and his body was never found."

"Wow, that's really something. I'd forgotten that euthanasia used to be illegal. What do you think happened to him?"

"I don't know. I suspect he had some sort of accident in prison, and the authorities wanted to cover it up. I can't believe they couldn't find him if he escaped. I'm not sure what I hope to find here, but I have to try. My father's personal library is at the Welcome Center for a reason."

Sean stood and they started toward the library. They stopped at Garcia's tomb and read the inscription:

President Jesus Renaldo Garcia
"Inside our great citizenry we shall find our
country's salvation."

"No one knew he meant it literally," Sean said.

They turned and walked the length of the mall to the library. They made their way up the massive steps and stepped into the cool quiet.

They stopped at the visitors map inside the entrance to get their bearings. To the left was the Hall of the First Term. Straight ahead was the Hall of the Second Term, and to the right was the Hall of Energy Independence.

"Is this place full of SPEYES?" Sean whispered.

"Actually, it isn't. It technically is not part of Central Iowa Farm. It's run by the National Archives and Records Administration and is independent. I asked that question when I started at the Tracking Lab."

Sean led the way straight ahead. The Hall of the Second Term was a circular, high-ceiling room with smaller 'themed' rooms spoked off the center. There were hundreds of photographs and video displays on the walls. Oak tables held computers for use by researchers and visitors. Across the way a man and woman stood looking at a video screen, while their two children chased each other around the tables. A young man who looked to be of college age sat at one of the computers. One of the side rooms was devoted to the second term presidential race, and Sean and Baxter entered it.

Sean stopped at a large video display. A sign identified it as the "Great Debates," and there, larger than life size, was Sean's father debating President Garcia. Sean felt a great sense of deja vu, as he remembered sitting with his mother watching that very debate when it was happening live. His throat felt thick, and tears welled in his eyes.

Baxter glanced at Sean and put his hand on Sean's shoulder. "I remember watching this in my American history class," Baxter said. "Our professor polled the class afterward to see who we thought won the debate. It was the consensus that Garcia won on style but your father won on substance. It was a good lesson on what counts in our society."

"My father didn't carry a single state." Sean turned from the display and looked absently around the room. "He was never the same after the election." Sean sat down at a research computer and typed in *Senator Duncan*. There were links to hundreds of items. "I might be a while."

"No problem," Baxter said. "I'm going to check out the Hall of Energy Independence."

Sean wasn't sure what he was looking for. He had done a lot of digging in the past, trying to uncover the truth about his father's disappearance. He had found nothing beyond the official government reports, and everything he found on this library computer was more of the same except for a handwritten letter from Senator Duncan to President Garcia, a copy of which had been scanned into the electronic archives. The senator had written it the night of the election, after the results were obvious. Seeing his father's flowing script on the screen gave Sean a chill. The letter congratulated the President on his re-election, and said he looked forward to working with Garcia in the coming years—standard stuff.

But the final paragraph surprised Sean.

While I disagree with your ideas for the way forward for our country I do hope that you are proven right in the end, and your ideas bring us to a place of peace and prosperity. Time will be the judge. If I live long enough to witness the results you predict, I will be among the first to toast your success.

Sincerely,
Darius

It was hard for Sean to imagine his father toasting Garcia for any reason, let alone the popularity of the Farms. But an objective observer (something Sean wasn't) would have to say his ideas were a success – still are. They achieved energy independence for America, and that resulted in the collapse of Big Oil and the need for the Never-Ending War. Better to fatten up for Uncle Sam than to die for him. Still, the letter didn't jibe with Sean's memory of his father's vehement opposition to Garcia's policies, and his vow to continue his fight against them.

Baxter roused him from his ruminations. "Sean, you've got to see this." There was urgency in his voice. "I think I found out what happened to your father."

CHAPTER 13

A FARM FUNERAL

After Sean and Baxter had left, Eden tried to put them out of her mind and prepare for the funeral service in the morning. She had provided the mortician with a set of clothes for her parents and found a black sweater of her mother's to wear to the service. She hadn't brought anything to wear to a funeral.

The service for Eden's parents was scheduled for 10:00 a.m. The small chapel was on the main floor of her building. It was softly lit, and several vases of fresh flowers were placed around the room. Eden had requested a Lutheran minister to say a prayer and read a couple of her parents' favorite passages from the New Testament.

She entered the chapel at 9:45 and walked up to the railing in front of the caskets. There was no way to get by the railing without climbing over it. The previous day's conversation with Baxter came back to her in a rush. Her parents had the right clothes on and certainly looked dead. Why couldn't she approach the caskets and kiss them goodbye?

A short Obie, dressed in ministerial vestments entered via a side door. He had a doughy face and an ill-fitting hairpiece that made him look like old, fat Elvis. "Good morning Ms. Sprayberry. I'm Reverend Thomas. I am so sorry for your loss. Please take a seat and we can get started honoring your parents. Do you have any request for a hymn or a prayer?"

"I want to kiss my parents goodbye."

"I'm sorry. That's against Farm sanitary rules."

"Excuse me?" Eden felt her blood rise. "Since when is touching an embalmed body unsanitary?"

"I'm sorry Ms. Sprayberry, but I have no say in the matter. I just follow the rules."

"Yeah, well bullshit." Eden sat on the railing and swung her legs over. An alarm sounded and Reverend Thomas tried to grab her arm. Eden reached out to touch her mother's hand.

It wasn't there.

Eden screamed. "You son of a bitch!" Eden's scream echoed in the small chapel as she slid back over the railing and punched Reverend Thomas in the face. Then she grabbed a vase of flowers and flung it against a picture of Jesus.

"Baxter was right!"

Two guards rushed in and wrestled her to the floor, handcuffed her, and led her out.

CHAPTER 14

THE
PRESIDENTIAL SUITE

The Hall of Energy Independence was a celebration of the Farm System, the New American Health Act, and, of course, President Garcia. In this hall was a detailed history of every step in the planning, building, populating, and operating of Garcia's big dream. Central Iowa was the first of the farms, and it was the focus of the exhibits. Every step in the creation of Central Iowa was recorded in ultradef video, and all the videos could be seen here.

"I was poking around the old videos and remembered what you said about your father's books being in the Welcome Center." Baxter and Sean sat close to the large computer monitor. "I found videos of the Welcome Center under construction. It was the first building to be finished. Except it wasn't always the Welcome Center. It started out as living quarters for the first Farm inhabitants."

"Yeah. So?" Sean said.

"So, they had a ceremony when the first busloads of people showed up. Come on and watch."

Sean stood behind Baxter as he brought up a video showing smiling fat people climbing off a big red, white, and blue bus. There was a ribbon cutting and speeches, with President Garcia doing most of the talking. Baxter skipped ahead. "Now look in the background." While the celebration continued, a white vehicle could be seen between the first two buses. It stopped in front of the new building. Two men in suits got out and opened the back door. A single man got out, and for a brief instant, looked right at the camera. Baxter paused the clip. Even in ultradef it wasn't easy to make out the face, but when Baxter zoomed in Sean could see the resemblance.

"Holy shit. That's him. It's got to be." Sean stared at the image. "What happens next?"

Baxter restarted the video. The three men disappeared into the building. Two minutes later the two in suits came out. One of them walked around the buses and joined the group of dignitaries milling about the freshly cut ribbon. He found Garcia and whispered briefly in his ear, then left. Baxter stopped the video and looked at Sean. "What do you think? Could he still be alive?"

"That was twenty five years ago. He'd be 82. So, yeah, he could still be alive. I can't believe he is. He would have let me know."

"If they let him," Baxter said.

Sean's head hurt. "Back it up to the three men again." Sean studied the screen. "Who are you Baxter?"

"What?"

"There are thousands of hours of video here. How did you know to look at this one? How did you find this 15 second section with my father on it?" Sean grabbed Baxter's collar with both hands and got in his face. "Who are you?"

Baxter took hold of Sean's wrists and pulled them off.

"Calm down, man. I'm just Baxter. Baxter the nerdy engineer. After I realized that these guys recorded everything, I thought I might be able to see something relating to your father's library. Maybe there was a dedication or something. It was just dumb luck. Honest."

Sean sat down. "I'm sorry. It's just all so crazy." He put his face in his hands and tried to make some sense of what he had just seen. Did his father come willingly? No, he had to have been a political prisoner. But why? He couldn't have been a threat to Garcia's big plans. The voters rejected him, and the Central Iowa Farm had become a reality. Why bring the library? Did they care about his comfort? How long did he live? Is he still alive? How did he spend his time? Sean sat up. "If you want out, you'll have to go by yourself. I can't leave here until I find out what happened to my dad."

"I'm having too much fun to leave yet. Besides, you're going to need my technical expertise. Have any idea of where to start?"

"I'd like to start in the Welcome Center. Go through every one of my father's books to see if he left any notes. Maybe there's a basement full of surveillance disks dating back to the beginning. But I don't know how we'd get in there to look around."

"It's empty at night. Everyone leaves at five. Disable the alarm system and cameras and break in."

Sean shook his head. "You make it sound so easy."

"It won't be. We can think about it while we see if there's any more information in this library."

"Let's check out Garcia's digs," Sean said. "Everything is supposed to be the way it was when he died."

They took the elevator to the penthouse of the Garcia Presidential Library, sharing it with the family of four they had seen earlier. Mom held on to her children's hands, trying to get them to stand still for the five second ride. The door slid open, and the children shot out into a vaulted, circular great room, where they continued chasing each other around the oversized furniture.

Sean stepped out and stood silently, while he looked around, trying to get a feel for the place. The floors were polished oak. A dark leather sofa and recliner sat on a huge circular rug with the Presidential Seal woven into it. They faced a massive entertainment center to Sean's left. Five arched, wooden doors, four of which were open, led off into other rooms. A set of glass doors opened into what must have been Garcia's office. It held an oak desk and two chairs. There were photos on the desk and walls. Sky lights in the domed ceiling let in the filtered sunlight. One large window provided a view of the mall. Only this window, two chairs, and a small round table that faced it were roped off. Signs asked visitors to please stay off the other furnishings.

There was a desk next to the elevator door that held a small rack of pamphlets describing the Garcia House. Sean slipped one into his pocket. A large, uniformed guard overflowed the chair behind the desk. She was asleep, her arms resting on her massive gut. Sean watched her open one eye when mom yelled for her offspring to be quiet.

"Nice place," Baxter said.

"Not as fancy as I thought it would be," Sean said. He walked to the window. "Hey, check this out."

Baxter joined him and read the sign next to the velvet rope. President Garcia had died in this chair, his half-smoked cigar, shrunken and dry, lay in the ashtray, his scotch glass next to it. Sean stared out the window. Across the mall, over the reflecting pool, the great statue of Garcia stared back. "Too creepy. Let's look around."

They toured the kitchen and guest rooms. Nothing interesting there. The last open door led to the master suite. It was here that some of the President's personal life was on display. The den off the bedroom held a writing desk. Its walls were covered with photographs. Sean and Baxter took their time, looking at each one, looking for Senator Duncan. He was in none of them.

"What happened to the First Lady?" Baxter asked.

"Died in childbirth. He never remarried. Their daughter survived."

There was one framed photograph on the desk. It was a wedding picture. President Garcia stood grinning next to Juanita, his daughter, and her new husband. Sean said, "Son of a bitch."

The groom was a much younger Sam Hawley.

"Nepotism is alive and well," said Baxter.

"He knows. He must know. I'll have to have another talk with him."

"You'll probably have to hold a gun to his head."

Sean smiled. "You got a gun?"

The sugar hyped children ran in, and Sean and Baxter walked out. "Well, what's the plan?" Baxter asked. They stood in the great room unsure of their next move. Mom and father were taking in the Presidential death chair. Their kids found them and tugged at their sleeves.

"We're hungry!"

"We'll be going in a minute," father said.

"I wanna go now!" The girl stomped her foot and pouted.

"What's in here?" The boy ran to the closed door, turned the handle, and pushed. The sleepy guard displayed more speed than Sean thought she was capable of when she leaped up and ran to the door.

"No one's allowed in there!" She grabbed the child's arm and pulled him back, slamming the door behind them. "That's supposed to be locked."

"Come on kids. Time to go." The family got in the elevator and father pushed the down button. As the door slid closed, the little boy said, "That room smelled funny."

CHAPTER 15

LUNCH

Back outside the two men began walking while keeping an eye out for the OP.

"No way do we go back to the car. It's probably gone by now anyway," Sean said.

"I'm really hungry," Baxter said. "Any place around here to eat?"

"There's a Freeburger about every mile. I'm hungry myself."

They were making their way back to Building 60, nearly backtracking the route they used to get to the library but skirted the abandoned car location. The two walked slowly in silence, sweating in the afternoon heat. Sean's head hurt. The insanity of the Farms, Central Iowa Farm, now had a personal element, a mystery that needed explaining. Getting the truth about a 30-year cover-up would be tough in normal circumstances but doing so with no resources while on the run seemed damn near impossible.

"There's a Freeburger up ahead," Sean said.

"Do you want to eat inside? Get out of the heat?" Baxter rubbed his hand across his forehead, then on the side of his leg.

Sean shook his head. "Too risky. ultradef TVs on every wall, all tuned to the Farm Channel. Someone would recognize us. We'll just use the Walk-Thru."

The Freeburger they came upon was shaded by mature oaks. It was in a transition zone between the city and one of the prefab neighborhoods. Freeburgers were just that: small fast-food restaurants (owned by U.S. Burger) that handed out free food to anyone who ordered. The choices were limited to burgers, French fries, oversized sodas, beer, and water. You could get your burger with bacon and cheese. Most everyone did. A sign next to the order window said PUBLIC DRUNKENNESS IS FROWNED UPON.

Sean and Baxter both ordered the Farmer's Special: two double bacon cheeseburgers with a half-pound of fries and a 32-ounce Capitol Cola. The outside seating consisted of reinforced concrete picnic tables and bench seats supported by four-inch steel pipes. A ton of citizenry could safely sit on each one. They both sat on the same side of the bench, backs facing the CCTV camera on the building.

Baxter slowed down halfway through his second sandwich, and after most of his drink was gone, he burped long and loud. "So, what's the plan?"

"Jesus Christ Baxter, I still don't know what the plan is." Sean made a face and set his drink down. "God that's sweet. I'm going to get some water." He went to the Walk-Thru window and returned with two bottles of cold water. The label said, "Farm Fresh-Recycled".

Sean handed a bottle to Baxter and said, "Sorry, man. I don't know. I thought we'd go back to Eden's and see what makes sense. She's leaving in two days, and it would be nice to hitch a ride out of here, but I'm not sure I can leave without learning what happened to my father. There's no history of it outside this place – no record. But the truth is here for sure. It's a reason for me to stick around. Maybe even cooperate. Shit, that's a thought."

"Let them catch you or turn yourself in?" Baxter asked.

"You think it's a good idea?"

"I think we'll both be in solitary feeding pens, fattening up for a suctioning, before we ferret out anything. It's your call obviously. Could you put up with this place for however long it takes to find the truth? Could I?" Baxter twisted the cap off the water bottle, took a sip and poured some over his head.

"Why would you want to hang around? I'm sure Eden would give you a ride out."

Baxter drank the remaining water. "You probably won't believe this... yes you will. My life before Central Iowa was pretty damn dull. I really didn't have any social life, no guy friends, no girlfriends. Get up. Go to work. Come home. Play fantasy computer games until I went to bed. Get up and do it again. Of course, here it's pretty much the same, except I don't have to worry about bills, cooking, or cleaning. Easy for me to get used to. I've had more real fun and excitement in the last 24 hours than I've had in the rest of my life. If I did manage to get past the border, I'd have to hide out from the Obesity Police, find a job, find a place to live. Don't get me wrong. I don't want to spend the rest of my life here, but when I get out, I'd like a clean slate." Baxter looked up at Sean. "You're the closest thing to a friend I've ever had. I'd like to help."

"They'll split us up," Sean said. "How do we stay in touch?"

"Not sure. After we pay for our escape and keep our noses clean for a while, I'll find you. It should be easy if you start shilling for the Farms. I'll probably lose my job at the lab, but who knows? Maybe I can convince them that I have some ideas on preventing what we just did."

"Well, let's think it over for a day." Sean got up and dumped the remains of his lunch in the proper receptacles: FOOD, PAPER, PLASTIC. Baxter did the same.

It was dark when Sean and Baxter made it back to Building 60. They came around the back and approached the parking lot with caution, scanning for security vehicles. There were none. Eden's Honda looked as if it hadn't been moved. The apartment balconies were empty – the residents opting out of the night's oppressive humidity. Most of the balcony doors glowed and flickered with the light of ultradef televisions.

"Let's get it over with," Sean said as he started toward the entrance.

CHAPTER 16

RECLUSE

On the penthouse floor of the Presidential Library, in the great room with the view of Garcia's tomb, the visitors had long gone, the main lights were out, and the gray twilight lingered for hours under the summer permacloud blanket. Four floors below, a great diesel's low throb, like the heartbeat of the devil, echoed through the cooling grates, driving air conditioning compressors that never stopped.

Outside, the President Garcia Mall was devoid of visitors save for the pigeons and squirrels that hopped around scrounging for their next meal. Garcia's statue was permanently lit by the LCD lamps that increased intensity as the daylight faded. Garcia had insisted on an eternal flame, ala President Kennedy. It was fed by a small pipe carrying biodiesel fuel and could be seen flickering in the distance. Other lighting winked on as well and the eclipses of moths began their nightly assaults on the glowing bulbs.

The fifth door, the only closed one, the one the little boy tried to enter, opened without a sound. A short figure, wrapped in a thick robe, shuffled out into the room. He carried a glass of scotch and an unlit cigar.

He walked around the velvet rope and stood for a short while at the window, watching the nature show below as the evening progressed. A half hour passed before he sat down in the chair opposite the President's. He lit his cigar and blew the smoke toward the empty seat. And, just as he had done every night since his friend's passing, he felt the sadness of loss, the melancholy of fond memories. *I'll be with you soon my friend*, he thought.

The door of the elevator opened and a uniformed guard on his nightly rounds emerged. He approached the small table.

"Are you okay sir?"

Without turning, the old man said, "Yes. Yes I am, thank you."

"Good. I'll see you tomorrow then. Have a good night, Senator Duncan."

CHAPTER 17

AN AGREEMENT

Sean and Baxter approached Building 60 carefully. The parking lot was devoid of people, and they didn't see any police vehicles. They made their way to the Sprayberry apartment and tapped lightly on the door. No answer. Sean tried the door, surprised to find it was unlocked.

"Maybe they were expecting us," Baxter said.

The apartment was empty, save for the keys to Eden's Honda. "Somebody cleaned this place out in a hurry," Sean said. "Wasn't Eden. She would have taken the keys and her car."

"You're right. At least whoever did it left us the vehicle," Baxter said. "Want to make a run for the border?"

"They'd never let us get out. They left the keys for a reason. I'm sure they expect us at the Welcome Center first thing in the morning. Besides, we can't leave without finding out what they did with Eden. And there's the unfinished business about my father."

"There's also the business about dinner, a shower and a good night's sleep," Baxter said. He opened the refrigerator. "Sweet. They left the food and beer. I hope they don't roust us out in the middle of the night."

"I'm betting they won't," Sean said.

The following morning the two men showered, shaved, and climbed back into their grubby clothes. After a breakfast of pancakes and sausage they headed for the Honda.

Sean drove, and Baxter rode, silent most of the way to the Welcome Center. Neither had slept particularly well. Sean wondered if he had any bargaining power left. Baxter knew that getting his old job back was out of the question, and wondered what they'd have him doing. Eden's Honda was a decent ride. The MPG indicator showed they were getting 55 miles per gallon of biodiesel. Sean turned on the Air Conditioner and watched the reading settle at 50 MPG. He turned on the headlights and watched it drop to 47. The little three-cylinder engine was straining now.

For his part Baxter felt like a too large ham in a too small tin.

"Maybe we can ask to be roomies," Baxter said.

"We can try."

A police vehicle had pulled in behind them soon after they left Building 60 and followed them to the Welcome Center. The two policemen didn't speak as they escorted Sean and Baxter into the building. "Stay in touch," Baxter said as one of the policemen directed Sean through an open door. The door slammed before Baxter could hear Sean's response.

"This is getting tiresome Mr. Duncan." Director Hawley sat across the same oval table in the same room with the book lined walls. "I'm considering placing you in our maximum security prison where after a few weeks you'd wish you'd taken me up on my offer."

"I had a chance to think it over. I will accept your offer, but with a few stipulations." Sean sat down.

"You're hardly in a position to negotiate," the director said.

"Probably not, but I won't do you any good locked up."

"What is it you want?"

Sean got up and pulled a book from the shelves. It was "Truman" by David G. McCullough. He opened the front cover and placed it in front of the director. "These books belonged to my father. They were in the house I grew up in. I want to know how and why they are in this building on this Farm." Sean didn't mention the movie clip, thinking the revelation might be put to better use later.

Director Hawley stared at Senator Duncan's signature. He arose and pulled another book from the shelf and checked it. Then another. "I don't know," he said, shaking his head. "I truly don't know."

"I find that hard to believe coming from the director of the Central Iowa Farm and son-in-law of the late President Garcia."

"How did you know that?" Director Hawley asked.

"Baxter and I visited the Presidential Library yesterday as part of our sightseeing excursion. Pictures of your wedding were in Garcia's den."

"Do tell. That surprises me since he never thought I was the right man for his daughter. And she thought then that the Farm system was an abomination. She's come to tolerate it since it's provided us with a good living. I'll have to visit the old man's library someday."

"Like you've never been in it." Sean smiled.

"Never have. Not even when the old man was still breathing. The library is not part of the Farm. It's managed by the National Archives and Records Administration and is run totally separate from the Farm. I have nothing to do with it. Juanita refuses to go there. Too many bad memories I guess." Director Hawley sat down. "So, what is it you need in exchange for your endorsement?"

"First I want to know what you did with Eden."

"She's safe and sound. We moved her in case you and your friend had any hostage taking thoughts. She has been sentenced to some jail time, but I think she might get out early if she behaves herself. She became extremely upset at her parents' funeral. Seems she had to touch them. Seeing her hand pass through their holographic images made her a little crazy. She kept screaming "Baxter was right" or something like that. Your friend Baxter has a good eye." Sam Hawley stood up. "By the way, we'll be impounding her car."

Sean doubted she would get out early. Holograms for bodies and bodies for the energy stream were things not generally known outside the Farms. All perfectly legal under the law, but no sense giving people another excuse for not joining a Farm if they are otherwise so disposed. "I'd like a job in this building, and I'd like Baxter to work with me. I'm not sure what kind of work you have here, but if that's possible I'll cooperate with the endorsement business. I'll even plump up and go in for one suctioning. Baxter is not a flight threat. He actually likes it here. He and I have become good friends in a short time and working with him would make my stay here a little easier." Sean paused. "One more thing."

"What's that?"

"No more butt chips," Sean said.

"I'll think about it. But why this building?" the Director asked.

Sean looked around at the books. "It seems like a good place to start."

Baxter was given a technical support job for the Welcome Center complex. Sean was assigned to Public

Relations. His first weeks were taken up with photo shoots to be used on the billboards soon to go up across the country showing a smiling Sean Duncan enjoying the good life at Central Iowa.

They were each given the keys to small apartments in the same complex near their work. When Baxter was given the news in his solitary cell, he wept tears of joy and relief. And when he first saw Sean again, he gave him a bear hug worthy of the largest of bears.

CHAPTER 18

THE BASEMENT

Sean soon fell into a daily routine of work, eat, sleep. Weekends consisted of ultradef TV, beer, food, some reading and no exercise. He was packing on the pounds and would go in for a suctioning in a month or so. He was apprehensive, but the knowledge that it was routine for so many people made him think it wouldn't be too bad. That lasted until Baxter went in for his first fat donation.

Baxter came home 50 pounds lighter with a lot of saggy skin and in a foul mood. He said it was different than he expected. He was sore and tired and didn't want to talk about it. He just told Sean that he would see soon enough. Baxter didn't want to spoil the surprise. Sean thought that Baxter's optimistic outlook suffered some permanent damage after the event.

Sean spent his lunch hours researching the history of Central Iowa Farm. Most of what was available was online and most of that was propaganda. Sean knew that the Eco-Thugs were still quite active at the time the Farms were being organized and built in the mid-50s. The New Luddite party had joined forces with the ETs, and their attempts to disrupt the US Internet were successful enough to cause a return to paper records and old-fashioned data storage for a short period of time. The New Luddites quietly disappeared after every one of their political candidates was assassinated weeks before the first presidential election of the new Farm era. The assassins were never brought to justice. The Eco-Thugs never ran for office.

Once a week Sean used his lunch hour to explore the Welcome Center building. He was somewhat of a celebrity now and everyone knew him on sight. The older employees interested him the most. Some of them may have been there from the beginning. But he found no one who had been. He was given a small office and a computer on which he composed cheery press releases and wrote "Sean Duncan's Farm Blog." He played his role and steadily gained the trust of the director. Occasionally Baxter would be in his building and would stop by to chat.

On one occasion Baxter had some news. "I had to go into the basement to inspect and repair some wiring. While tracing the cables I came across a locked storage room. It had a sign that said "RECORDS". The lock looks easy enough to pick."

"I haven't explored the basement yet," Sean said. "Of course I want to get into that room. Problem is we'd need to do it on a weekend. Or maybe you could gain access and leave it open. I could check it out during my lunch hours. Where is it in relation to my office?"

Baxter told Sean how to find the records room and said he would open the room that afternoon. If an alarm sounded Baxter would say the door was unlocked when he opened it looking for any more cables and wiring. There were no alarms that afternoon. Later that evening Sean and Baxter got together for a few beers.

"How did it go?" Sean asked. They were in Sean's

apartment, a one-bedroom efficiency similar to the one he had had at Farm Jail, only smaller. All the food, beer, wine, and booze were the same.

"No problem. Old fashioned lock. I went in and looked around. If any place has what you are looking for it's got to be there. It's a real mess though. Lots of filing cabinets and boxes, both marked and unmarked. I don't think any-one has been in there in years." Baxter finished his beer and opened another.

Sean leaned back in his chair and closed his eyes. "I wonder..."

"Wonder what?" Baxter asked.

"I think it's time for me to write the definitive history of Central Iowa Farm. I think Hawley would think it's a great idea. I could push it as a wonderful recruitment tool. Especially if I told him I could get it done in time for the Farm's 25th anniversary celebration next spring."

"Man, you're really sucking up," Baxter said.

"If he agrees then I could have access and all the time I need to go through the old records. I think he trusts me enough now. He rarely checks up on me anymore. Nor has he mentioned my father. I think he's been too busy worry-ing about the declining crop yields to even care." Sean leaned forward. "But from what I hear the ad campaign featuring Sean Duncan has done wonders for enrollment."

"Why do you think we need a history book?" Sam Hawley barely looked up from his screen when Sean pro-posed the idea in Hawley's office the following morning.

"Another recruitment tool, human interest, something to sell at the visitor center."

Hawley looked up at Sean. "I don't care. Just don't let it get in the way of your real job."

"Is there somewhere that stores old records and photos?" Sean asked.

"Much of that went to Garcia's library," Hawley said.

"Mind if I poke around in the basement? Maybe there's some old records and paperwork down there."

"I haven't been down there in years. But, sure, help yourself."

"Thanks."

Sean got the access he wanted and at the first opportunity made his way to the records depository.

Baxter had understated the room's disarray. It was a chaotic assortment of cabinets, boxes and shelves which filled a room of about 30 by 40 feet. There was little room to get around, but thankfully Sean found the lighting adequate. Where to start?

Sean began by clearing out a corner in the room and stacking any boxes with dates later than those he was interested in. Anything around the Grand Opening plus or minus two years would be the first things he would look at in detail. After several hours he had three file boxes, one filing cabinet, and a section of shelving that fit the bill. With a lot of sweaty effort, he transferred the files in the cabinet and the material on the shelves to boxes emptied of uninteresting files he dumped in the corner. By quitting time, he had managed to get all of the material moved to his office. He had barely scratched the surface of the records room contents.

After an evening of too much wine and a night of too many weird dreams Sean sat in his office and began the task of sorting through eight boxes of history from Central Iowa's beginning years. It went fast since most of the material was of no interest or importance: invoices, quotes, check stubs, stacks of printed emails that shouldn't have been, time sheets, meeting notes, construction photos – nothing related to Sean's search. Useless paper. Whoever predicted the paperless office didn't predict the $29.99 color printer or people's continued love of "hard copy".

Time for another fishing expedition in the basement.

Sean was into his fourth day and third load of boxes when a notice appeared on his OED that someone wished to see him. He pushed the "Allow Access" button. Two minutes later Eden Sprayberry was at his office door.

"Eden. What a pleasant surprise." Sean arose to greet her, but his attempted hug was rebuffed. She looked tired and resolute, thinner than Sean remembered her. What had it been? Four or five weeks?

"I'm leaving this shit hole," Eden said. "But I couldn't leave without telling you just what a disgusting prick you turned out to be. And you're fat too."

"They locked you up, didn't they?"

"Yes, but it didn't prevent me from seeing your ridiculous ad campaign and reading your stupid blog. How could you?"

"It's not what you think. Besides, it was your ruse that got me here." Sean plopped back into his chair. "Please sit down for a minute. Let me explain."

Eden hesitated but sat down across the desk. She looked around at the piles of musty documents with a quizzical expression. "What are you doing?"

"Remember I told you my father's library was...is... in this building?" Sean said. Eden nodded.

"When Baxter and I left your apartment that day we went to the Presidential Library as planned. Baxter happened to be watching a video of this Farm's grand opening ceremonies. In the background a white limo pulled up and three men got out and went into the building. This building. One of them was my father."

"Are you sure?"

"Pretty sure," Sean said. "Anyway, my capitulation was the only way I stood a chance of finding out the truth. This pile of stuff is from an old storage room in the basement. Hawley granted me access when I told him I wanted to write a history of Central Iowa in time for the 25th anniversary next year."

"Have you found anything?" Eden asked.

"Nothing yet, but there's a lot more material down there to go through. Want to help?"

"My bus leaves in an hour. I really need to get out of here."

"Why did they lock you up?"

Eden fought back a tear. "After I ran my hand through my parents' bodies and knew they no longer existed I went nuts. Punched a minister and elbowed a guard in the eye. Tore apart the chapel pretty good. I got 60 days. Got out in 30 for good behavior. They never even apologized." Eden waved her hand. "Enough of that. It's done. How's Baxter? You guys in touch?"

"I got him a job here too. We live in the same apartment building. He's doing okay. Went in for his first suctioning. I don't think he's been the same since. I'm due to go in a week or two."

"Did he say how it was?"

"He wouldn't tell me. He said every newbie should be surprised."

Eden got up to leave. "If there's anything I can do to help on the outside let me know."

Sean stood. "I wish you wouldn't go. I could use you here."

"Doing what?" Eden gave him a skeptical look.

"Research assistant. Assistant editor. I'll think of something. What are you good at?" Sean smiled.

"I have a degree in public relations, and I was damn good at it." Eden sat back down. "What are you good at? Besides gaining weight?"

"Ouch. Look, this is a one-shot deal. And despite the promotional ads I'm still opposed to these fucking farms." Sean sat on the edge of his desk. "I actually have a degree in constitutional law, but I never really practiced. I studied law to please my father. He hoped I'd follow in his footsteps someday."

"Why didn't you?"

"No fire in my gut. Lost it after my father was jailed by the country he loved. I got a job as a teacher and half-assed joined the resistance. Tried to live quietly. Worked well until the Obesity Police started sweeping neighborhoods unannounced. When you found me, I was on my third visit to a safe house."

Eden stared out the window. "Are you getting it now?"

"What?"

"A fire in your gut."

Sean started to speak but stopped and walked to the window. After a minute he turned to Eden. "I want to burn this place down. Not sure how to go about it. How about you? Did your funeral experience light a fire in you?"

"I'm still pissed, and I doubt I'll get over it anytime soon."

"Then stay here and help me figure out how to exact our revenge."

"I'll need a job and a place to live."

"So that's a yes?"

"Yes, and by the way, I know what we need to do."

Sean said "That was quick. What is it?"

"You need to run for president. I'll be your campaign manager."

"You're kidding, right?"

"No, I'm not. It just came to me in a flash. You now have nationwide exposure due to your stupid Farm System billboards and pop-up internet ads. You don't need much money since politicians no longer jet around the country. Older folks will remember your father, many had voted for him—twice. If we... when we win, we'll shut these damn farms down for good."

Sean sat back down. "It sounds crazy to me," he said.

Eden got up to leave and turned back to Sean. "Think about it."

"I will. Meet me at the Garcia library at noon tomorrow. We'll talk about it."

CHAPTER 19

RUN SEAN RUN

Ever since the great farm migration the presidential elections were won by the candidate that promised to maintain and improve the farm system. The millions of farm inhabitants always tipped the elections to those who would allow them to continue their chosen lifestyle. In addition, voting was a requirement for anyone who lived and worked on a farm system farm.

The historical two main political parties—neither of which were a majority of the population—evolved into the pro-farm Republicans on the right, and the anti-farm Democrats on the left. Republicans loved taxing the Obies either by collecting their fat or their money. The Democrats wanted the fat tax repealed and the collection of human fat to stop. Most of the population was unaffiliated with any party, and many didn't care one way or the other. The Rexics and Indies weren't single issue voters and many didn't bother voting at all. The resistance didn't vote, especially the Obies, since all votes were traced and verified so that a vote would guarantee they'd be found and arrested for tax evasion. The Independents in the resistance voted with the DEMS due to their overall disgust with the whole farm/fat issue, but none of it mattered due to the millions of guaranteed votes from the fat and happy Obies at the farms.

All of this whirled in Sean's head as he lay awake the morning after Eden suggested he should run for president. He thought of the two campaigns his father had run and how expensive and tiring they were. He knew campaigns were very different these days, as much of society's human interaction had evolved into virtual contact. Political contests evolved as well. Sometime mid-century they had become pure video affairs. Contestants debated virtually nonstop over the various social media platforms. It was rare to get two opponents in the same room debating live, but it still happened, and it made for must-watch TV. Who won or lost these debates was decided on social media and almost instantly. It became an online shouting match that was almost as popular as the Super Bowl as millions of viewers expressed their opinions while others upvoted or downvoted their comments. Some compared it to the lions and the Christians. Thumbs up—thumbs down.

Sean wondered if would be possible to run a campaign from Central Iowa Farm. Money wasn't an issue—it was possible to run for office without the need for millions of dollars. Social media accounts, websites, email bots, and the constant American desire for the latest 'thing' could make a campaign go viral for no apparent reason. Voting was entirely online, yet some of the population still didn't bother due to their distrust of the system. Hacking, or attempted hacking, of an election was punishable by a very public execution by hanging. The few that had occurred were the most watched TV in history. Sean had watched one out of morbid curiosity. He threw up afterwards.

His thoughts went back to Eden. What he really wanted to do was to bed Eden in the short term. Her volunteering for campaign manager gave him hope. Sometimes human urges crowd out other considerations. He was very pleased that she decided to stay and was sure he could add her to his "team" dedicated to writing the history of the Iowa Farm. Hopefully he could get her an apartment in the building he was in.

After a quick shower and some coffee, Sean called the office of the Director and asked for an appointment. He could be seen at 10:00 AM.

The conference room door was open, and Hawley motioned him in.

"Good morning Mr. Duncan." Sam Hawley remained seated.

"Good morning Mr. Hawley." Sean sat down across from the desk. The smell of the old books in the conference room caused Sean to breathe deep and gather himself.

"What brings you here on this fine day?"

"I'd like to know my status. Seems to me I'm working in some Public Relations capacity in exchange for room and board. Right?"

Sam looked at his computer and scrolled down the file. "Pretty much. We've had good recruitment following your PSAs. Enrollment is increasing. How is the history book progressing?"

"That's why I'm here actually. I'd like to add an assistant. There's so much material that I'm afraid I won't be able to finish in time. It won't cost the Farm much, just use of an empty apartment. And, before you ask, I want to hire Eden Sprayberry. She's still pissed about her folks, but she said she'd help."

"Really. You two are a thing now?" Sam smiled.

"Not yet, but I'm working on it. She's sharp. Alright with you?"

"See HR and let them know. Just get it done—and with the right slant."

After Eden left Sean's office, she went to a Freetel, a free hotel room reserved for visitors who had requested a tour of the farm with the expressed desire to find the right farm for them. Iowa Farm wasn't too popular, but the west coast Farms were hard to get into. The waiting lists were long.

Eden hadn't slept well. She spent hours flopping around on a lumpy mattress thinking about her conversation with Sean the day before. She wondered if he was attracted to her. She wondered if what she was feeling was anything more than her long running, unplanned celibacy. She finally got out of bed at nine, showered, and got dressed in jeans and a turtleneck. She liked the way she looked in it and hoped Sean would like it too.

Sean was waiting for her on the library steps when Eden's robocab dropped her off.

"How'd it go?" Eden asked, giving Sean a brief head-turned hug.

"You're my new research assistant for the history of Iowa Farm. I've asked HR to find you an empty apartment. I should hear by this evening. Let's grab some lunch." Eden led the way up the steps.

The Presidential Library cafeteria, not being part of the farm, charged for meals—reasonable prices for decent food. They bought the food from the farm; a good deal for both. Eden ordered a salad and water. Sean ordered a Buffalo burger with French fries and a 16-ounce craft beer. At the register Sean waved his OED over the Pay Here display.

"Are you earning money here?" Eden asked after they took a seat in a window booth.

"I have a small expense account that I negotiated when I accepted the promo offer. Not much but it allows me to buy you lunch today."

Eden looked at Sean's plate when it arrived. "Are you really going to get your fat sucked out?"

"I have to. I can't be the voice of the resistance unless I know all about what I'm resisting. And, if for some reason I do decide to run for president, I'll need all the ammunition I can get. I saw what happened to Baxter, but I need to experience it myself to see what it's really like. I think it will strengthen my resolve."

"I didn't think you'd take me seriously," Eden said.

"Were you serious?"

"Sorta. I really want to fight this bullshit. I will help if you're serious. This will take a lot of thought and planning. Will your friend Baxter help?"

"Let's find out," Sean told his OED to set up a meeting with Baxter that evening. After a slight pause Sean smiled and nodded at Eden. "He's good."

Baxter met Sean and Eden at Sean's apartment at seven. It was pizza and beer for dinner as the meeting got underway. Baxter did a quick scan for bugs – finding none.

"How far off is the next Presidential election?" Baxter asked his OED.

"12 months and 2 days." Answered the device.

"That's a start," Sean chuckled.

"Campaigns don't start in earnest until a couple of months before election day," Eden said, "so we have some time. I think the biggest issue, if we decide to campaign from here, is getting good access to the World Wide Web."

"There are computers on the farm that have access," Baxter said, "but I haven't tried to hack into them yet. I'll make that my first priority."

"I'll begin working on our platform," Eden said, "I'm assuming we're campaigning as Democrats?"

"The acorn doesn't fall far from the tree," Sean smiled.

"That won't work," Baxter said. "The Dems will have a candidate all picked out with a ton of money to spend on the campaign. Our only hope is to run as independents — maybe come up with a new, unique party name. Something to capture the imagination of the lazy, uninterested populace. How about the NOBESE party? Our motto could be 'WE DON'T SUCK."

"Good one Baxter. But I agree," said Sean. "We should run as a new party. NOOBIES?"

"Our platform will be very similar to the existing DEMS," said Eden. "I like something simple, like "THE NEW DEMS" or some such. Whatever we decide we'll have to do a search on the existing party names. There's a ton of them out there."

"Well, be thinking about it. We have some time."

The brainstorming session went on until Baxter declared himself ready to turn in due to it being a workday eve. Eden took notes, but much of the time was spent trying to convince each other it was possible to run, without giving much thought to whether it was possible to win.

"Let me know when the next meeting is," Baxter said. "Have a good evening."

"You too, Baxter."

"Oh shit," Sean said, "I never heard from HR about your lodging. Did you check out of the Freetel?"

"Yes, I did. All my belongings are in the hall."

"I'm sorry. I should have called. You can have my bed. It's clean. I'll sleep on the couch."

Eden got up and stood before Sean. "Pretty sneaky. You never called HR. But that's okay. I've always wanted to sleep with a fat guy."

CHAPTER 20

WILL'S REVEAL

By late afternoon the next day, Sean was in the records room for the fifth time. He felt a renewed sense of urgency. The night before, with Eden, was excellent. He didn't even feel bad about lying. He had gotten a text from HR while they were eating lunch, but conveniently forgot to mention it.

This morning, they made love again, in the shower. After he dried off and wrapped himself in his towel, he went out to make coffee. His OED indicated a message from HR. It said the apartment was ready for Eden to move in. While the coffee was brewing Sean stood in the bathroom doorway and watched as Eden did her hair. "We should do that more often," he said.

Eden smiled. "Get. Get dressed and go to work."

Sean shook off his pleasant memories and got back to work.

He had made it through the easy and obvious containers, coming up empty handed so far. He stood in the silence, leaning against the gray painted concrete block wall, wishing that something in what remained would magically start glowing and pulsating, showing him the way to the truth. He had thought it would be easy, that there would be a magic document that explained it all in terms easy to read and understand. He had visions of bounding up the stairway, charging into Director Hawley's office waving the evidence. *Where are you hiding him?* He would scream. *He's got to be here somewhere.*

Sean shook off his vision. *There is still a chance that some-where in this forgotten room such a document exists. There is still a chance my father is alive somewhere in this crazy complex, this vulgar enterprise, this new American Farm.* He reached up and pulled an old cash box from a high shelf. It wasn't locked and was full of old thumb drives. He put the box in his stack to be reviewed later. The top shelves were beyond his reach. His previous attempt to climb on stacked boxes resulted in a dangerous fall, which left him bruised but otherwise unhurt. Today he went looking for a stepladder.

The Welcome Center basement was large and unre-markable. It contained the usual basement stuff: furnaces, water heaters, electrical breakers, maintenance supplies. There was a maintenance room, complete with an old metal desk where sat an older, gray-haired man. He was of slim build and wore a yellow jumpsuit. He seemed to have all his teeth and much of his hair. Sean did not recall seeing this person before and had a momentary vision of a troll under a bridge.

"Good afternoon," Sean said, extending his hand. "Sean Duncan."

"Good afternoon to you, sir," the man responded. "I know who you are. I'm Will, Will Washington."

"I haven't seen you around before. You stay pretty much down here?"

Will smiled. "Yes sir. I just keep the equipment running

for the most part. No need to get upstairs. I'm only part time these days. They call me in when they need something fixed."

Will's face was deeply creased, and his hands looked strong, but his fingers were gnarled with arthritis. Sean guessed him to be in his late seventies at least. The maintenance office was clean and orderly. The desktop was empty save for a laptop and printer. Above it was a bulletin board with some work orders pinned to it. There was also an old-fashioned printed calendar that was twenty-four years old. The month was June, and the photograph was of the new Welcome Center building. A shot of adrenalin made Sean's heart pump faster.

"Will, that's an interesting calendar. Have you been here since then?"

Will turned and looked at the calendar. He was silent for a moment. "A year before actually. I guess I probably have the most seniority in this place. I found my niche, you might say."

Sean's stomach hurt. "Do you know who my father was?"

"How could I not know? It was all over the news."

"Did you ever see him in this building?"

"Not recently," Will said through a half smile.

Later, after calling Eden to see how her move-in went, Sean stopped by Baxter's to tell him about Will and what Will was able to remember.

"He said he was one of the original hires – 44 years old in 2059, when Central Iowa began adding staff. He hadn't worked in years and jumped at the chance at a job at Central Iowa. Jobs on the outside were still scarce so the competition for Farm employment was fierce. President Garcia insisted on hiring those people who had been without work the longest. Will fit the bill and was hired as a maintenance worker as soon as the new building had electricity. The Grand Opening was six months later. Will and the rest of the crew spent weeks spiffing up the grounds. There was a lot of excitement as the day approached. Everyone wanted a glimpse of President Garcia. His approval rating was 100% on the Farm – he had given everyone there a new job, new hope for a brighter future.

"I asked him if he remembered seeing the white limousine drop off my father and he said he hadn't. But he did remember seeing who he was sure was Senator Duncan supervising the unloading of crates of books on the loading dock. When he mentioned it to his boss, he was told that his job would disappear if he ever talked of it again. Senator Duncan had escaped from prison and was never found. End of story.

"Will didn't mention it again, but neither did he forget it. He had been a Duncan supporter and voted for him in both elections. He reflected that idealism and hunger sometimes are at cross purposes."

"I've seen Will once or twice when I had work to do in the basement," Baxter said. "Never had a chance to stop and chat."

"Back then the Welcome Center was the first housing unit for the Farm. As a maintenance worker he had access to all the apartments save one – the Presidential Suite. President Garcia lived there for a while between leaving the New White House and moving into the Garcia Library. After the move the suite was the first apartment to be converted to offices. Will worked on that project and one of his jobs was to move all the books. He opened a few as he put them on their new shelves. But he kept his mouth shut.

He was convinced my father lived there and moved when Garcia did."

"Wow," Baxter said. "That's incredible. How did they manage to keep it a secret?"

"There are things the government can do, and does do, that we mere mortals can't even imagine. Loose lips sink ships, and all that. If your lips are loose, they'll cut them off – at the neck. And Will is a simple man who really needed his job. Not one to rock the boat."

"So what's your next move?" Baxter asked.

"We have to spend some quality time at the library. Will didn't think I'd find anything in the old records. Garcia was too thorough. "Sean opened two more bottles of beer and filled their glasses. "But first I am due for my suctioning. It's scheduled for next Friday."

"That's good. You'll survive. I did. Friday is the best day to get it done. You have the weekend to recover." Baxter took a long draw of the cold beverage.

"It's crazy," Sean said. "Most people don't have a choice about recovery. They just go back to their apartments to begin packing on the pounds again."

"It was tough on me. The day after they extracted my fat, I was offered a choice of special treats. They do this to donors, depending on their desires and habits. I've heard that some get German beer, others single malt scotch, and still others *pate de foie gras*. It's supposed to shut us up about the discomfort and raise our caloric intake right back up to a maximum. Most donors, I think, get stupid drunk afterwards. I did."

CHAPTER 21

TAX DAY

On the Thursday before Sean was to give up his fat, he sat down with Director Hawley to update him on the history project. Sean had returned all the files back to the document room with no effort to leave the place as he had found it. He thought he would be the last person to visit it until some future gung-ho administrator realized there was a fair amount of potential energy in all that paper and sent it on to the energy stream.

"I've pretty much concluded that most of what I need to move forward on my book resides in the Garcia library. I found some old documents in the basement, but they didn't help at all," Sean said. "With your permission I'd like to spend next week there doing my research."

"Yes, I suppose most of the information would be there," Hawley said. "Did you come up with any explanation for the books?"

Sean shook his head. "Not yet. I know the government confiscated anything of value after my father was incarcerated. Who knows? Maybe Garcia wanted them as some sort of memento." Sean arose to leave. "By the way, I'm visiting the Fat Man tomorrow, so I won't be in to work."

"Good luck. Let me know how it goes."

First time fat donors received special treatment. Sean was instructed to shower with the antiseptic soap that was left outside his door overnight, and to dress in the red jumpsuit that was in the same bag. Sean was picked up promptly at noon by Robert, a member of the bioteam, commonly known as the Lard Squad. Robert wore an off-white jumpsuit. He would be staying at Sean's side throughout the whole process and bring him home afterward. Robert made small talk on the drive to Building 20, the closest building with a collection room. Building 20 was similar to Building 60 and Sean wasn't surprised when Robert led the way to a first-floor elevator and pushed the down button.

The first thing Sean noticed was the smell. If he had to describe it, he would say it was a strange combination of sweat and bacon grease, maybe a little sweeter. When the elevator door opened it really hit him. He almost gagged.

"You get used to it after a while," Robert said.

"I doubt it," Sean said.

They were in a hallway with a tiled floor that gleamed in the LED overheads, a checkered pattern of beige and light green. Shining stainless steel double doors lined both sides, spaced forty feet apart. Above each set of doors was a light that was either red or green. The hallway seemed to extend forever.

"You can go into any door with a green light," Robert said. "They're all the same."

Sean fought the urge to fight his way out, but suspected Robert was well prepared for that possibility. He didn't want to be asleep for his first "payment". He didn't want to be awake either. He didn't want to be down on the collection floor at all, but he couldn't carry on the fight, or write an honest book, without firsthand knowledge of what the good people of Central Iowa Farm were going through. The thought of losing 50 pounds of fat in an hour was hard to imagine. *Did it hurt during? Afterward?*

Four doors down a lamp went from red to green, and the double doors opened. A man in a wheelchair emerged, pushed by an orderly. The man's eyes were closed, and he wore a tight-lipped grimace. His hospital gown was stuck to his torso with sweat. Sean tried not to stare as the wheelchair passed.

Sean pushed his way through the first set of doors with a green light. He had been expecting a small, personal chamber, but instead the doors opened into a gigantic hall of gleaming stainless tables and pipes and machines. Beds stretched as far as he could see. Most were occupied by donors. Robotic arms moved like spider legs above the beds, controlled from a room high above the floor. The remote-controlled liposuction machines hummed softly, filling the cavernous area with a beehive drone. Sean broke a sweat. The temperature had to be 95 degrees Fahrenheit at least. The smell was overpowering. An occasional moan could be heard above the hum.

Sean turned to ask Robert why all these people didn't seem to mind the lack of privacy when Robert poked him in the arm with a small needle. In an instant he was as happy as he had been since he was brought to the Farm. He looked up from where the needle had stuck him and grinned a stupid grin and giggled. "Robert, my man, let's do this!"

Sean remembered all of it: The leather restraints that held him tightly in position, the paralyzing effect of the "happy" shot, the gleaming, articulated arms of the fat-sucking robot, the intermittent whir of the pump pushing his contribution down to the main collection pipe. It seemed like an eternity, but lasted only forty minutes. When the shot wore off the discomfort set in. He was nauseated and weak. His belly sagged in his lap. The wheelchair ride back to the car and the subsequent ride to his apartment seemed to take forever. Robert helped him into bed. He slept for sixteen hours.

He awoke before dawn with a slight headache and an overall feeling of soreness. The steamy shower felt wonderful. The two-stitch incisions pulled a little. Sean brushed his hair and teeth without looking in the mirror. Maybe later he thought. He got dressed in a loose sweatshirt and shorts. He wouldn't be going anywhere for the next couple of days.

He was hungry, but nothing sounded good to him. He drank a small glass of cold water and lay down on the sofa. He dozed off for a bit until there was a slight knock at the door. He struggled to his feet and shuffled to the door. When he opened it he found a large gift basket in front of his door. There was expensive wine, brie, baguettes, chocolates, smoked sausage, and a thank you card from Central Iowa Farm. "Unbelievable." He shut the door and went back to the sofa.

The next knock was louder. "Door's open," Sean said as loud as he could.

It was Baxter. "You sound like shit. Here's your goodie basket. I'll put it on the kitchen counter." His voice was way too cheerful to suit Sean's mood. "You're looking especially lousy. How did it go?"

"You know damn well how it went, you bastard. You could have warned me."

"What? And spoil all the fun? Knowing ahead of time

would have just made you more tense. Besides, they say the first time is the roughest. It's supposed to get easier the next time."

"There won't be a next time," Sean said. "I'm getting out after I find out what happened to my dad."

"That's right. You've paid your debt," Baxter said.

Sean walked into the kitchen and opened the refrigerator door. He closed it and looked at Baxter. "Make yourself useful and cook me some breakfast."

Sean dozed on and off all day after Baxter left. While awake he watched some college football. His alma mater was showing some promise this year, so he did have some interest in their game. It had been decades since every college game in the country could be seen on some satellite channel. It didn't matter the size of the school or the meaninglessness of the game, it was available for viewing. Even the small schools made money since the rules were changed to allow for advertising on every available arena surface, including the player's uniforms.

Later Baxter stuck his head in Sean's door. "How are you doing? Feeling any better?"

"Come on in. I'm feeling better, thanks. Been snoozing mostly."

Baxter grabbed a chocolate from the goodie bag and sat on the sofa across from Sean. "So, when are you going to the library again?"

"I'm spending next week there. Too bad you have to work. I could use your research luck."

"What happens after you leave? What if you don't find anything?"

Sean shut off the television. "I won't leave until I find something. After that I plan on making sure the history gets rewritten to reflect the truth. That's probably a nearly impossible task since most people won't give a shit. I'll do the best I can. After that I want to work on getting these Farms shut down. What they do to people is disgusting – inhuman even. I'm glad I went yesterday. It made my mind up for me. No one should go through that even if they go by their own free will. Another impossible task I'm sure, but people on the outside will know the disgusting details. Hawley won't like the new billboards I plan on doing."

Baxter got up to leave. "I'll leave you alone now. Get some more rest. You're going to need it."

"Thanks. Oh, and take the rest of those chocolates with you."

CHAPTER 22

DISCOVERY

By Monday morning Sean was feeling good enough to go to the Garcia library to start his digging. Public transportation was free. The small, smelly buses were on time and ran frequently. He grabbed a tote and put in some cheese, an apple, and a bottle of water, then took the ten o'clock to the library.

During the twenty-minute ride he tried to formulate a plan to search in an organized and meaningful manner, but he knew he would begin in Garcia's penthouse. What Sean wanted was time alone there, without the guard. Perhaps there was a place to hide until the library closed and the guard went home for the night. He would just have to play it by ear. He tried hard to remember all the details of the visit he and Baxter had made a few months ago. It was the half observed and peripheral things he tried to remember, knickknacks, the guard's response to an open door, the child's comment about the room smelling funny. He remembered nothing he thought would be of use. The bus clattered along the long, straight roads, stopping for anyone who flagged it down and wanted aboard or who was aboard and asked the driver to be let off. Sean closed his eyes and feared he would find nothing. As his doubts grew, so did his anger.

The bus dropped him off at the library steps. He sat for a bit and ate his apple, then went inside and used the restroom before riding the elevator alone to the penthouse. Few people, if any, were in the library. He didn't see anyone in the entryway or in the great halls. He smiled at the guard as he passed her desk. He thought it was the same woman but couldn't be sure. Sean's nerves were on edge, and he felt a heightened sense of awareness as he scanned the room. *Use all your senses, Start with your eyes.* Sean scanned the room slowly. *Anything different? Out of place? Then your ears. Any sound out of place? Unfamiliar?* The deep thrum of the basement diesels was more felt than heard. *Now your nose. Close your eyes and breathe slowly. Parse the smell. Old books. Cleaning solution. Cigar. Yes.* Sean's eyes popped open. He detected the faintest odor of cigars. Faint, but real. He looked at the shriveled cigar butt laying in the ashtray on the table between the two large leather chairs. That hadn't emitted any odor in decades. He walked over to the guard and asked, "Do they allow smoking in here?"

"Oh no sirree sir. No one can smoke in the library. Don't even think about lighting up."

Sean smiled. "I wasn't going to light up. I just thought I smelled a cigar. Probably not."

"Whoa!" The guard struggled to her feet; eyes wide. "You know. Some mornings when I come in, I think I smell a cigar. I asked my supervisor once. He said it was just the smell from the air conditioners and dehumidifiers. I hadn't thought about it until you mentioned it."

"I suppose that's possible," Sean lied. "What time do you close?"

"Five o'clock. I'm out of here at five oh one." She laughed and sat down with a heavy thud. She got right back up. "Shouldn't have sat down. Gotta use the restroom."

Before she closed the door to the public restroom in the hallway Sean said "Have a great night. I'm on my way out."

"Okay sir."

Sean took the elevator back to the main floor to while away the hours until late afternoon. He spent the day searching for more film clips that might show evidence of his father's presence, but he found none.

At 4:45 Sean took the elevator back to the penthouse. The guard's head was down on her arms. She was sound asleep. Sean quickly tiptoed past the desk and into Garcia's glass-walled office. He sat on the floor behind the big desk. He couldn't believe his luck. At five o'clock the guard's OED played the national anthem. Soon the lights went down, and the elevator doors opened then closed. The hum of the diesels was all Sean heard. When his eyes adjusted to the dimmed lights Sean found that he could see quite well. He stood and opened the center drawer on the desk. Typical stuff. Left hand top – a box of cigars, cigar cutter, and a butane lighter. Sean lifted the lid expecting to see some old, dried sticks, but they seemed to be fresh based on their appearance. He picked one up and squeezed it, smelt of it, definitely not that old. Who was smoking these? The guard? The maintenance crew?

Sean was startled by a soft sound. He slid the desk drawer shut and looked around. He identified the sound as coming from a door outside the office—the one that no one was allowed through. The door cracked open, and Sean ducked behind the desk. From his position he could only see the legs and feet of whoever came out the door, shuffling slowly. When he thought it was safe to peek, Sean did. The adrenaline rush almost made him pass out. Senator Duncan, his father, in the flesh. The outside door to the main room opened and Sean ducked back down. "Are you okay Senator Duncan?"

"Yes. Thank you," in a quiet voice.

Sean waited until the outside door closed and avoided rushing out, not wanting to startle his father. Instead, he waited until his breathing and heart rate were almost back to normal. He entered the main room slowly. His father was sitting in one of the leather chairs, a lit cigar in one hand and a glass of whiskey in the other. An overhead exhaust fan had kicked on sucking the cigar smoke up and out. The fan was quiet, efficient. Sean sidestepped slowly until he was behind his father, his reflection clear in the darkened window.

"Hello son."

Sean was overcome. He began to sob softly; the tears were a hot flow down his cheeks. He didn't approach until he had regained some control. His father stood, and they embraced for a long time. Sean spoke first.

"Oh dad, dad. What happened? What is going on? Why are you here? What?"

"Come and sit with me son. Garcia's not here to kick you out of his chair."

Sean went over to the guard's desk, grabbed a tissue, and blew his nose. Then he joined his father behind the velvet ropes and sat in the president's chair.

"Would you like something to drink?" the senator asked.

"I would like an explanation. What happened to you?"

The senator took a sip of his whiskey. "First, I must say this is such a blessing to this old man. I was hoping we could reconnect before I died. I've been forbidden to make contact with the outside since President Garcia pardoned me. For my freedom I had to promise not to badmouth the Farm System and swear an oath of secrecy. I would have given up and died years ago if I had to stay in that prison. God knows I wanted to let you know, but I was afraid, weak. I wasn't sure if you had forgiven me for giving your mother her wished-for peace. I'm sorry Sean." The senator began to cry.

"Dad, you can explain the details later. Don't apologize. I've always respected you for what you did for mom. But what's important now is that I've found you. How do you feel? How's your health?"

"I'm feeling pretty good for a man my age. I'm treated well; good food, good health care, TV, books, the World Wide Web – though it's filtered and monitored. How have you been son?

I knew you were at a farm. I saw the pop-up ads and pictures of the billboards. I didn't know you were at Central Iowa, but I hoped you were."

"I got turned in to the Obesity Police and arrested for failing to pay my fat tax. You might appreciate that. Anyway, I was assigned to Central Iowa Farm Jail. Got busted trying to escape. I made a deal with the director to do the farm promos in exchange for getting out of jail. I still had to pay my tax. Three days ago I went in for a suctioning. Worse experience of my life. I'm more determined than ever to see these farms shut down. But now I just want to get you out of here. How can I reach you? Do you have an OED?"

Senator Duncan shook his head. "I'm not leaving. I am comfortable, and as I said, well taken care of. President Garcia saw to that. But yes, you can reach me." The senator pulled his OED from his left front pocket and held it up. Sean retrieved his and the ensuing beeps indicated that the devices were now known to each other.

"But dad, I can take care of you. I want to be able to see you every day. In person."

Senator Duncan shook his head. "This place isn't like the Farms. We can video chat. Don't be upset. Very few people know I'm here. Like I said, it was a requirement of my freedom that I tell no one, not even you. I expect after tonight they will know that you know. Might get interesting. We'll see. I would ask that you sign an NDA when asked. I do not need a press of reporters demanding to interview me." The senator puffed on his cigar and sipped his whiskey. "I'm sorry son, are you married? Any kids? My WWW filters wouldn't allow that information through."

"I was married once, but it didn't work out. She loved the whole farm idea and moved to a California farm. No kids, fortunately. I do have a new lady friend here, in Central Iowa. I'll introduce you as soon as possible. Her name is Eden. I've also made a very close friend. His name is Baxter. Nice young man. You'll be meeting him also."

"I'm looking forward to it." The senator set down his whiskey and his cigar and promptly fell asleep.

Sean had a hard time digesting it all. He sat and watched his father sleep, listened to his gentle snoring, and finally dozed off. He awoke to his father tapping him gently on the shoulder.

"You had best be going son, my guardian will be here soon to check up on me and bring me breakfast."

Sean stood and tried to shake off the sleepiness. Senator Duncan gave his son a hug. "Do what you must do, what you believe in. We'll talk more soon." He entered his room and closed the door behind him.

Sean felt a hollowness and he wept softly. The sound of the elevator door brought him to attention, and he went and hid behind the president's desk again. The guard went directly to the senator's door and went into the suite. Sean hurried out and took the elevator down. Let the guard scratch her head over the elevator not being where she left it.

On the bus ride back, Sean called Baxter. "Can you talk? We need to talk."

"Not now. I have to go to work."

"Call in sick, or say you'll be late for some reason."

"No can do. I'm off at five. Come over then and I 'll buy you a drink."

"Thanks. Will do."

Sean got back to his apartment feeling emotionally drained. He was exhausted, but excited to tell Eden and introduce her to his father. He made a piece of toast and ate it with a glass of milk. When finished he lay on the sofa and fell asleep.

Sean slept until three, showered, shaved, and ate a small salad. He received a message from Baxter saying he got home early, and Sean could come by.

"What can I get you?" Baxter asked.

"A glass of red works. Thanks."

Baxter poured two glasses of merlot and waited patiently for Sean to speak.

"When you didn't come over last night with a report on your day's research, I figured you must have found something big," Baxter said.

Sean took a long sip of wine. "I found my dad Baxter. I

found my dad. He's alive. He has a suite off of Garcia's in the museum."

"No shit? That's incredible. What...how..."

"He's been living there since Garcia moved there. In exchange for my father's freedom from prison my father agreed never to speak ill of Garcia or the newly proposed Farms and to stop the campaign he launched in prison to have the New American Health Act repealed. My father consented mostly because he simply could not stand being in prison. He said it would have killed him if he had had to stay there. Turns out Garcia contacted him about a possible deal when my father's campaign got a little traction and some intrepid reporters started digging into the "health" act."

"So can you get him out?"

"He doesn't want to leave. Says he's comfortable and well taken care of. He has Web access so we can "see" each other whenever we want. Turns out he and Garcia became close friends and enjoyed many a cigar and glasses of scotch together before Garcia died."

"So what now?" Baxter refilled their wine glasses.

"I don't know. I've got to get out of here eventually, but can't stand the thought of leaving my father behind."

"How is his health?"

Sean gave Baxter a sideways look. "He seems to be in good health… for his age. Not likely to die soon if that's what you're getting at."

"Oh no man. I was just curious. He may outlive my fat ass the way I've been eating and drinking. Does Hawley know?"

"Actually, he doesn't. Turns out Garcia never liked him, and Garcia's daughter hated the Farms and the fact that her father was responsible for them. He said he's never been to the library, and I believe him."

"You going to tell him?"

"I doubt it. Very few people know about it and I'm afraid of the consequences for my father if Hawley knew. What a mess." Sean got up from his chair. "I guess I'll sleep on it and see if a path forward becomes clear. Good night Baxter."

"Goodnight."

CHAPTER 23

ANOTHER GARCIA

Sean woke early and lay in bed sorting through his thoughts. He'd love to get his father out, but what could he offer him? Certainly not a more comfortable life. His issue was access and the feeling that he needed to rescue him. Of course, he wanted to go back as soon as possible to spend time with him and to get more details on how he came to live with his presidential rival. He also wanted to talk to whoever it is that's taking care of him. He especially wanted information on his health and what was to happen after he died.

He felt that the best approach was a direct one. Go talk to the library director and tell him who he was and what he knew. After a quick breakfast and shower, he was on his way back to the Garcia library.

At the service desk in the library Sean introduced himself and asked to see the director.

"Do you have an appointment sir?" the pleasant lady at the counter asked.

"No I don't, but please tell him Sean Duncan would like a few minutes of his time."

The young woman took her OED into a back room to make her call. She was back in a minute and smiled. "He'll be right down."

The director of the Garcia library was an older man of medium build. His name was Pedro Garcia—a distant cousin of the former president. He led Sean to his second-floor office by way of a staircase off the main lobby. The office was large and exquisitely furnished, complete with a wet bar, wine cooler and humidor. The ceiling had large, quiet exhaust fans.

"Would you like a cup of coffee, cocktail, cigar?" the director asked.

"I'm good. Thanks." Sean walked around the large office studying the photos on the wall—construction scenes of the library and President Garcia's monument.

"It's a pleasure to make your acquaintance, Mr. Duncan. You're quite well known outside Central Iowa farm. I've been expecting you ever since your talk with your father."

"How did you… shit. A SPEYE, of course. Why wasn't I told? I've been here since last September for Christ's sake." Sean could barely conceal his anger.

Pedro Garcia got up, poured himself two fingers of scotch, and retrieved a cigar from the humidor. He flipped a switch on the wall. The large, silent fans began to rotate.

"I am bound by a non-disclosure agreement signed by my great uncle and your father. I chose to honor that agreement since I am a man of my word. Your father didn't know of your presence at Central Iowa because we filtered his internet access." Garcia lit his cigar and blew a smoke-ring toward the ceiling. "I understand your anger. Now that you know where to find him, you're welcome to visit at any time… after you sign a nondisclosure agreement."

"My dad said you'd ask, but I'll do no such thing. Some

people still want to know the truth." Sean stood up and glared at the library director.

"It is your father's wish. He doesn't want the resultant bedlam should his circumstances become public."

"Give me a scotch," Sean said.

Pedro Garcia poured a double for Sean.

Sean downed the drink in one gulp as Garcia placed the NDA in front of him. Sean signed the agreement and stormed out of the office.

When Sean got back to his apartment he called Baxter. "Can you come over this evening? We need to talk. I'm asking Eden to come too… six is good. Thanks."

Next he called Eden. "Hello Eden. Can you come by at around six? Baxter's coming. We need to have a meeting. I'll fill you guys in this evening. Thanks. See you then."

Eden arrived first and she hugged and kissed him before saying hello. Sean was pleasantly surprised.

"Um, thank you. I needed that."

"I wanted that," Eden said.

Baxter arrived soon thereafter, and Sean put a frozen pizza in the oven while Baxter retrieved some cold beers.

"Thanks for coming over on such a short notice. I met the library director today. His name is Pedro Garcia, distant cousin of Jesus Garcia. Turns out he knew I found my father."

"You didn't think they'd be SPEYES in that penthouse?" Baxter asked.

"Jesus Baxter, I hadn't seen my father for twenty-five years and you expect me to think about SPEYES?" Sean shook his head. "Turns out it didn't matter. He made me sign a nondisclosure. I pitched a fit, but it didn't matter. My dad had asked me not to tell a soul, so I signed the

NDA. I'm going to see my father tomorrow. I want to give him some idea of what we plan on doing, so let's plan on doing something."

Eden checked on the pizza and Baxter brought out two bottles of merlot. By the time the pizza was done the mood had loosened up. Sean went to the refrigerator and grabbed some raspberry cheesecake. "It's gonna be hard giving up this farm cuisine," Sean said, "Shit's wonderful."

"Yes it is," said Eden and Baxter simultaneously.

The three of them decided the basics of their platform over dessert. The main plank was the eventual dismantling of the Farm system. Everyone currently a non-worker would be grandfathered in and could stay as long as they wanted. However, no more harvesting of human fat would be allowed. The energy shortfall would be made up by a new effort to establish a foolproof nuclear energy capability as well as new research and development of battery technology not dependent on the precious metals being hoarded by the Chinese. All diesel vehicles were to be converted to EVs when such technology became available. Until then, biodiesel fuel would be made from the things that now went into making millions of people fat—sugars and fats.

Other planks were basically the standard liberal fare including free dental and optical care for citizens not on a Farm, free internet and streaming services, higher taxes on the rich, passage of the equal rights amendment, and a reduction in military spending. All three of them know they didn't stand a chance without some new, game-changing idea… but nothing came to mind.

Baxter said goodnight and Eden and Sean enjoyed some horizontal recreation before falling asleep.

CHAPTER 24

REUNION

Sean arrived at the library at four the next afternoon. He took the elevator to the President's suite and found the same fat, young lady at the reception desk. Sean pulled out his OED and brought up his pass. The guard scanned it and checked her screen. Her eyes grew large.

"Are…are you related?" she stammered.

"I'm his son."

"Your son is here to see you sir," she spoke into her device. She looked up at Sean, eyes still wide. "Second door on the right. Let yourself in."

"Thanks."

Sean pushed open the large door and found his father waiting with a smile. He was shorter than he remembered him from years ago, but trim and not stooped by time. He wore a baggy sweat suit with a University of Michigan logo on the front. His gray, thin hair still covered his head.

"Hello son. Thanks for coming up."

They embraced for a long minute before the senator showed his son where he lived. The suite was large and nicely decorated. It had a sitting room, large bedroom, decent size kitchen, and another large room, a den, which held shelves of books and several computers, as well as some state-of-the-art home gym equipment. Some windows had views of the mall. Sean took it all in with a combination of joy and sadness. He stopped at every picture on the den wall: pictures of his family when he was young, pictures of the senator at various events, a picture of his mother holding him as a newborn. Sean fought the tears and caught a sob in his throat. He gathered himself and said, "This place is huge. How did you swing this?"

"Jesus was very good to me. We became quite good friends. We spent many hours enjoying a cigar and good whiskey, discussing the same things we debated all those years ago. I miss him, but I really can't complain. What would you like to drink?"

"What are you having? I'll have the same." Sean sat in one of the den's leather recliners.

"Single malt with one ice cube. Sound okay?

"Absolutely," Sean said. He couldn't take his eyes off this old man, who was his father, who ran for president, who vanished from his life for over two decades. Part of him was pissed off at the deception and his father's un-willingness to contact him. But the main part of him was overjoyed to know his father was alive, and he was sitting in the same room with him.

The senator poured their drinks and set them on the table between the leather recliners.

"How are you feeling dad?" Sean asked after they relaxed with their drinks.

"Like I told you the other night, I feel pretty good for a man my age. I try to exercise a little every day. Great food, great health care, great respect from my guardians. Hard to complain. I complained at first, but when I saw what was happening in the U.S and around the world, how people were struggling, I realized that I had a sweet deal and could make it work. I keep myself up on current events and write in my journal every day. I have many essays that I wish could see the light of day, but it will never happen. Perhaps you'll want to read them."

"What are your essays about?" Sean asked.

"Before I answer, what say we order dinner? What would you like?"

"What are my options?"

"Pretty much anything."

Sean thought back. What did he enjoy as a kid? What was his favorite meal?

"I'd like some macaroni and cheese with chunks of Spam. Can you make that happen?"

"Absolutely. I have that about once a month. It reminds me of your mother. One of her go to meals when she was in a hurry." The senator tapped the screen of his OED. "Be up in half an hour."

"How hard was it?" Sean asked.

"How hard was what?"

"The decision you made about mom."

"The hardest thing I've ever done in my life. I would have traded places in a heartbeat." The senator wiped away a tear.

"I can't even imagine."

The arrival of their dinner broke the mood. As Sean and his father ate their meals, the talk turned to the Farm System. Sean started getting a little riled. The senator just nodded politely. When the meal was, finished Sean cleared the plates. When he returned from the kitchen Darius smiled at his son and said "Thanks for cleaning up. Now would be a good time for some brandy and a decent cigar. Please join me."

Sean hadn't had any tobacco since his college days but said, "Sure, okay."

The senator turned on the ventilation system and poured two brandies and retrieved two cigars from his humidor.

"When did you start smoking cigars and drinking brandy?" Sean asked.

"President Garcia got me hooked. During our long discussions he'd smoke and sip some kind of whiskey – sometimes scotch, sometimes rye, sometimes brandy—and I noticed how much he seemed to enjoy it. Then I tried some single malt and a good Cuban. I was hooked. Have you ever read Robert's biography of Churchill? Churchill drank every day and smoked cigars every day. It was estimated that he smoked 160,000 cigars in his lifetime. And he lived to be 90 years old. An amazing man."

Sean followed his father's lead and cut the tip of his cigar and lit it. He took a puff and coughed.

"Just don't inhale," the senator said. "Ninety percent out your mouth and ten percent out your nose."

Sean tried again then took a sip of his drink, smiled, and said, "I get it."

They sat in silence for several minutes.

"So, tell me about your essays," Sean said.

"Mostly my observations on why the farms became such a success. Some on current events. Nothing earth shattering. I'll send some to you. Are your emails monitored?"

"I imagine they are. I have a friend who is trying to get us access to the real Web. If he's successful I'll set up an account and let you know. The Farm Web is a joke."

"Interesting. I have access. You can set up an account right now if you'd like," the senator said.

"Why are you worried about someone seeing them?" Sean asked.

The senator poured them each another finger of brandy. "The powers that be are still worried about the fact of my existence. If I were to break my NDA I'd lose this comfortable arrangement. After all these years I doubt that anyone still remembers or cares."

"Well somebody does. Why do you think that is? Why did Garcia set you up like this? You two never did see eye to eye on his proposals. What was he afraid of?"

The senator sipped his drink and stared into the glass for a long moment. "When I was in prison, I started an "underground" newsletter designed to foment unrest among those who believed as I did and wanted to shut down the farms. It started to gather a following. To me it was more or less a hobby, something to keep me busy and sane. It kept me busy, but I still felt I was going insane. One day, without notice or explanation, I was taken to an offsite location and placed in a small, windowless room. I was scared, actually, but who should walk in but Jesus himself. I was quite surprised to say the least. That's when he made me the proposal that resulted in my present situation. He felt sufficiently wary of the underground support I was generating to offer me a full pardon and a comfortable life if I would shut up and behave. I agreed because I hated that prison."

Sean's eyes got wide. "Was your newsletter called *The Farm Plow?*"

"Yes, it was. How did you know?"

"Unbelievable!" Sean said. "I read those newsletters and joined the so-called resistance because of them! Of course you couldn't put your name on them, so I had no idea who was doing the writing. And, of course, that's why I too, ended up at Central Iowa. You were talking to me and didn't even know it." Sean got up and poured them each another finger of brandy. "I am so proud of you dad, and grateful for our serendipitous reunion." Sean raised his glass for a toast and the senator did the same.

"Who could imagine?" the senator said. "But I still don't think anyone cares anymore."

"A lot of people still care dad, a lot," Sean said. "After the farm start up sucked up all of those who wanted that lifestyle, the country remained close to 50-50 on whether they were a good idea. And, during the ensuing elections, the farm vote was all that kept the farms going. But you know that, I'm sure."

"Some of my writing touches on those issues and how the farms have affected the USA's standing in the world. Some countries have tried to emulate us, but only Mexico has come close. Some politicians have tried it in Canada, but it resulted in them closing their borders to US citizens to prevent the spread of the Obesity Police." Darius got up and started pacing. "You know… I wish I were a younger man. I'd run again. And I think I could win. Although the way elections are run these days, I'm not sure an old man would stand a chance."

"How about a younger version of you?" Sean asked.

"What do you mean?" asked the senator before a look of recognition took hold of his face. "Do you want to run for president?"

Sean smiled. "I do. My closest friends want me to. I have decent name recognition thanks to you and my bull-shit pro-farm propaganda. I want to shut the farms down. I went through a "harvesting." No one should go through that. I can't believe people keep doing it after the first time. The farms are disgusting. I want to shut them all down."

"How do you propose to run an election from Iowa Farm? Don't you need to travel the country?" the senator asked.

"I've paid my so-called fat tax and I'm free to leave, but I told director Hawley I'd do his promotional spots just so I could hang around and see why your library was at the Welcome Center. Then I told him I wanted to write a 25th year history of Iowa Farm so I'd have access to old records. He agreed. In any case the current president never left his estate when he won his first election." Sean stood and looked out over the mall. "It won't be easy, but with a little luck and a lot of social media access… well, you never know."

"I'll help any way I can, son" Darius said.

"Thanks." Sean turned toward his father. "I want you to meet Eden and Baxter. Baxter is my IT guy and Eden is my campaign manager. I wish it could be in person, but I had to sign an NDA. Are you allowed to leave the library grounds?"

"No, and I don't want to. When your friend gets a secure link to the real Web, we can meet on-line. Then I can share my essays and some thoughts I have on running your campaign."

"I gotta get going dad. Lots to think about. I'll let my team know we have a new member." Sean hugged his father and started to leave.

"Who'll be your running mate?" the senator asked.

Sean stopped and turned around. "I have no idea."

CHAPTER 25

A MEETING
OF THE MINDS

On the bus ride to his apartment, Sean messaged both Eden and Baxter and asked them to join him for dinner at his place. They both agreed.

Sean baked some frozen lasagna and made a salad. As they ate, Sean related the details of his meeting with his father. Both of them expressed a keen interest in meeting the senator and seemed thrilled that he was willing to help the election campaign.

"Any luck on getting us real Web access?" Sean asked, "We really need it soon."

"Since you just said your father has access, I'm beginning to think the Garcia library may be the place to hack into. From what I've seen so far, their spying and secrecy protocols are probably less than those of the Farms. I'll plan on getting over there this week and check things out. We could probably operate out of there if we wanted to. Pretty low visitor level typically."

"While you're there, see if they have reservable

conference rooms," Eden said, "We may be able to run an entire campaign from the Garcia library. That would be a coup. Maybe they're hiring. I'll check on that and if so, I'll apply."

"You want to go over there together?" Baxter asked Eden.

"Sure. Any day works for me."

"How's tomorrow at 10? Still got your Honda?"

"It's impounded. I'll summon a robocab and pick you up."

"Sounds good, you guys," Sean said. "Um…one thing. I need a running mate. Think about who. Meanwhile I'm going to have to bang out the history book I've been working on to keep the director happy and unsuspicious. Maybe just show him one chapter at a time until we need to go full out blitz with our campaign. What's your feeling about when we need to declare and start with the billboards and on-line ads?"

"Six months," Baxter answered.

"That may be too soon," Eden countered, "With the current American attention span we may want to wait until a month or two before election day. I'm serious. Elections are way different than they used to be. We'd just need to be totally ready to flood the country with our ads."

"I remember my dad's two campaigns," Sean said, "he spent all his time raising money and running around the country. Barely saw him those election years. It's definitely different these days."

"Yes it is," Baxter said. "Also, if we start too early we may get shut down just when we're attracting some attention."

"Sean, do you think your father would be willing to do some ads for us?" Eden asked.

Sean smiled. "I sure hope so. It would mean reneging on his NDA, but if he gets fired up enough, he may not give a shit." Sean got up and stretched.

Baxter also rose and stretched. "I'm out of here. Have a good night." Baxter let himself out.

"Care to spend the night?" Sean asked.

"I'll have to give you a rain check. I need a good night's sleep." She gave Sean a hug and kiss at the door and left.

Sean didn't get upset. His invite was perfunctory, and he was glad to be alone.

Sean lay awake thinking about everything. It was one thing to say you're going to run for president, it was another thing to actually do it, and with such limited resources. He decided to ask Eden to be his running mate since he didn't really know anyone else to ask. Good for the women's vote he thought. He hoped Baxter would lose some weight and join his administration too. Then he laughed to himself. *I'm thinking I'll win the election! And I haven't a clue how to actually go about it.* He let himself imagine it anyway—like buying lotto tickets—impossible odds, but buying a ticket also bought some pleasant daydreams.

At 10:10 the next morning Eden and Baxter rolled into a Patriot Fuel station to gas up the robocab.

"Why do we have to put fuel in a robocab?" Eden asked.

"We happened to get one that was low on fuel. Luck of the draw. It's free. No big deal."

"I hope I got some of my own fat in that tank," he said, sliding in.

"Oh, that's gross." Eden made a face as the cab pulled out and headed for the library.

Things were slow at the Garcia library. It was late autumn, not the busiest of seasons. Eden inquired about a conference room and was directed to the second floor, where there were several to choose from. She and Baxter picked one that had a decent view of the mall. The room was spacious, well lit, and had a large, oval oak conference table surrounded by eight chairs. A small computer sat in front of every chair. The two sat at opposite ends and opened the laptops.

"I'm looking for employment opportunities here," Eden said.

"And I'm looking for system vulnerabilities," Baxter whispered.

"Try not to crash it."

They worked silently for a while.

"I just applied for the position of National Outreach Coordinator," Eden said.

"Sounds important."

"It isn't. If I get it, I'll be trying hard to increase the visitor numbers. I should get an answer soon. I doubt if they have many applicants. How are you doing?"

Baxter looked up. "Good. The system is old and unsophisticated. But I'm going to need to bring in a more powerful machine to do what I want to do." Baxter stood up and stretched. "Hey, if you get that job you'll get an office and access to the real web. Else, you couldn't reach out. Let's hope they like your resume."

Eden's OED beeped. She picked it up and opened the screen. "Unbelievable. This place must really be hard up. I just got the job."

Baxter gave her a hug. "Tell them you want this room for your office and that you'll need a bigger computer."

CHAPTER 26

ELECTION HEADQUARTERS

The very next day, Sean, Eden, and Baxter stood in Eden's new office on the third floor of the Garcia library. It was larger than the conference room on the second floor where Eden applied for and got her new job. There was a dusty desk with dual monitors, an old computer on the floor, large table, comfortable chairs, and an empty wet bar. The office overlooked the mall through large wall length windows. A barren bookshelf lined the wall behind the desk.

"When's the last time someone worked here?" Sean asked.

"It's been a while," Eden said. "The position has had a half dozen occupants, but every one of them opted to re-sign and move to the Farm after a year or two. No one's held this position for five years."

"And no one's cleaned it since," Baxter said, drawing a smiley face in the dust covering the desktop.

"You didn't even have to interview?" asked Sean.

"Just a meeting with HR and a photo for my ID badge. There's a lot of "don't give a shit" going on here. But I get it. After years of no one visiting, people quit caring. It's the American response to so many things—give up and give in."

"Baxter, what do you think?" Sean asked.

"This is sweet. I'll have a look at that old computer and see if Eden needs to requisition a new one. I suspect she does. I'll also do a quick check for SPEYES."

"Anybody seen Pedro poking around?" Sean opened the office door and looked out into the hallway.

"I was introduced," Eden said. "Seems like a nice man. Brief chat. He doesn't seem too ambitious. I expect he'll leave me alone."

"So, what's next?" Sean asked.

Eden and Baxter looked at each other. "You're the boss, Sean," Baxter responded.

Sean sat down in one of the well-padded chairs and held his head in his hands. "I wish I had a plan. I don't. I'm going to talk to my father and see if he can point us in the right direction. Meanwhile, I need you two to research recent past elections to see what's worked and what hasn't." Sean got up and looked at his cohorts. "This is pretty crazy, isn't it?"

"Yes it is," they said.

"It may get crazier," Sean said. He smiled and looked at Eden. "I want you to be my vice president. And Baxter— chief of staff."

Baxter was speechless. Eden was not. "I know nothing about being vice president. Don't you have friends from law school?"

"Never made any friends in law school. It seems that a son of a liberal senator is persona non grata for the most part. But I believe you are more than capable. You might be the next Harry Truman."

"Let Baxter be VP and I'll be chief of staff."

"I'm a tech guy, not a politician," Baxter protested.

"Please think about it and decide which office you'd like. No way are we going to find anyone else in this place to run for office with me. Besides, it's not likely we'll win."

"Bad attitude, Sean," Baxter tsked.

Eden called library maintenance and asked that her office be thoroughly cleaned as soon as possible. "I'll order all the supplies I think we'll need to get this war room up and humming. Let me know if you have any special requests."

Baxter sat down at the desk and turned on the computer. An outdated login screen appeared asking for a username and password. "Eden, call the library IT guy and tell him you want a modern computer and login credentials. Tell him to order one if there's none available. Tell him you want the Googlesoft operating system installed."

Sean and Baxter were about to leave when library director Garcia walked through the door.

"Good morning, Eden, Sean, and who might you be?" he asked Baxter.

"I'm Baxter Bodecker, sir," he said, extending his hand. "I'm a friend of these two. Just helping Eden get started."

"And what do you do at the Farm?"

"I'm the IT guy at the Welcome Center. I was just telling Eden to call your IT guy and order a modern computer and operating system."

"Unfortunately, we haven't had an IT person for a couple of years now. Would you be interested in a little side work? If you have the time, of course."

Baxter suppressed a smile. "Sure. I can always use a little extra money. I could work Saturdays. Who do I see and what's my budget?"

"Go to HR with a list of what Eden needs and have them call me for my approval. After that do an evaluation of the library's system and put together an estimate of what we need to update everything."

"Will do and thank you sir," Baxter said.

"Nice meeting you Baxter. Good seeing you two," Garcia said, nodding at Sean and Eden as he left the office.

Sean closed the door and said, "Way to go you guys!"

"That was way too easy," Baxter said. "I like that guy. I'll get the new computer ordered right away. We should have it in a couple of days max. Also, no SPEYES."

CHAPTER 27

HISTORY BOOK

Two weeks after Eden started setting up her office, Sean finished the first draft of the history of Central Iowa Farm. He had Eden do a quick read and edit before he sent it along to Hawley. The two of them spent a week selecting photos to include in the book. Overall, it was comprehensive, but a little disjointed after he decided to run for president. He had hurried to finish after that, and the writing showed it. Since Hawley probably would only skim it or have a subordinate read it and send it out for publishing. Sean wasn't too worried. It was certainly accurate, somewhat well written, and better than nothing.

Writing the book was an interesting experience for Sean. He was surprised at how much he didn't know about the times through which he had lived. He was well versed on current politics and government policy — his father used dinner time (when he was there) to expound on current events and government with a teacher's touch and a late-night comedian's humor. But there was a disconnect from pop culture that Sean's father encouraged, albeit not overtly. Sean wasn't discouraged from social media, sports, or any other activities that a typical teenager wanted to do.

But the home environment eased Sean away from a lot of the frivolity that pervaded youth culture. He would rather read a book than be glued to a screen. Consequently, he wasn't always up on the latest social media platforms, memes, or teen speak. Law school was a reprieve from the pop culture information overload. He was with many who had been raised the same way he was. But his liberal father was not a favorite among the law school students.

Sean printed out a copy of his book and hand delivered it to Director Hawley. "I've got a present for you," he said, dropping the manuscript on his desk. "Hot off the presses."

"What is it?"

"It's the book, The History of Central Iowa Farm. I thought you might want to read it before I sent it to the printer."

Hawley picked up the document and looked at the cover. "It's heavy. I'll have a member of my staff read it and let me know if it's acceptable."

"Are you going to read it?" Sean asked.

"I know what's in it. What I want to know is what you're going to do now that it's finished."

Sean just shook his head. "Who's responsible for the Farm Channel? Any chance Eden and I could work for whoever puts it on? Maybe some specials or a daily news report? Last time I looked it was boring and repetitive."

"And how would that benefit us?" Hawley looked skeptical.

"The Farm Channels, all of them, are available for watching by all US citizens. I doubt if many of them do. Some interesting content that presents Central Iowa Farm in a contemporary and, perhaps, humorous light may bring in more visitors to check things out. Just a thought."

"Go down to the production studio and see if there's any interest. It's not a bad idea, actually."

Sean left with several new ideas spinning in his head. He knew where the production studio was since he had been there several times to shoot the promo ads for the Farm. He called for a robocab and had it drop him off at the library. He wanted to see if Eden was available to accompany him.

"Knock knock," Sean said, rapping on the door frame.

"Sean! What brings you?" Eden was at her desk working on Library business.

Sean stepped in and looked around. "This place looks great. It definitely needed a woman's touch. Anyway, I just delivered the book to Director Hawley. He's not going to read it of course, but will assign that task to one of his minions. He asked what I was going to do next, and I asked him if there may be some interest in making the Farm Channel more interesting to watch, and if so, could you and I get involved. He liked the idea after I explained that all citizens can watch the farm channels, and maybe more would if they were more interesting, and perhaps that would result in more curious visitors to Central Iowa. I'm on my way to the studio and wondered if you were available to tag along."

"It's almost lunch time, so yeah, I can go."

Holiday decorations were beginning to appear around the Farm neighborhoods. It was nearing Christmas and New Year's Day, a festive time at the Farms. Christmas Day was a special day of gluttony. Christmas Eve was just a warmup. Delivery trucks clogged the highways and parking lots for two weeks prior, as gifts and food were delivered to the waiting populace. Christmas week was "tax free", and no suctions were scheduled. The entire week between Christmas and New Year's Day was one big party. Fat production always spiked in late winter.

"Christmas at Central Iowa. I can hardly wait," Sean said.

"My folks always enjoyed it."

"I will too since I've got my dad to celebrate with. And Eden the Adorable."

"Thanks. I'll miss my folks, but I'm glad I have someone to share the holidays with." Eden got quiet for a moment. "So how do you propose to make the Farm Channel more interesting?" Eden asked, wiping a tear.

"Man on the street interviews, wildlife of the farm, restaurant reviews, etcetera. I'm sure we can come up with more fun stuff if we try. But that's not what I'm excited about."

"Go on."

"The fact that all of America can see the Farm Channels means that we will have access to the real internet. Once we get some political ads put together for our campaign, we can spew them out across the USA just before the election. With Baxter's help we can probably make them hard to take down right away."

"We were going to do that already – from the library's system."

"We still will but having them on the Farm Channel gives them an air of "Farm approval" if you will. For the Farm Channel ads, we won't mention that we want to end life as they know it. It just may swing a percentage of farm votes our way."

"You'll go to jail again," Eden said.

"Only if I lose."

The Farm Channel production studio was located on the main floor of one of the residential buildings several miles north of the library. It was a small area and took up only a small portion of the available space. There was a glass double-door entrance that led to a reception lobby. Jim James, the Farm Channel administrator, sat at the reception desk. Jim was a tall Rexic with a permanent look of amused skepticism on his face.

"Hello Jim," Sean said.

Jim looked up and smiled. "Hi Sean. What brings you here?" Jim arose and walked around his desk to shake hands. "Who's this pretty lady?"

"Jim, meet Eden Sprayberry. Eden, Jim James."

"Pleased to meet you, Eden."

"Same here Mr. James."

"Please call me Jim. And please have a seat."

Sean and Eden sat in the two chairs in front of the desk. Jim sat back down. "Does Hawley want you to do another bullshit ad?"

"Now Jim, you know I believed every word I said." Sean smiled.

"Uh huh. And I have some dry land to sell you in Miami."

"Actually, Eden and I would like to do some human-interest pieces for the Farm Channel. You know, to add a little reason to watch, spice things up. Hawley thought it a good idea and it wouldn't cost you anything except the use of this facility on occasion."

"Well, if I let you do that, I'd run the risk of losing my one claim to fame."

"What's that?" Eden asked.

"Having the most interesting shows on Farm TV. But, sure, absolutely. Studio's yours when you want it. Just call ahead to make sure it's available. I'm looking forward to seeing what you come up with. Keep in mind, nothing too edgy, lest the censors get their knickers in a twist."

"He sure doesn't seem like a dedicated Farm guy," Eden said. They were on their way back to the library. "Sounds like he thought your ads were a joke."

"Jim is interesting. I get the feeling he thinks the Farms are a joke, but he wouldn't say so directly. A sort of free spirit, that one. I'd like to approach him about helping us, but I'm not there yet."

"Best be careful."

"Oh, I will," Sean said, as the robocab pulled in front of the library entrance. Before Eden got out, he asked her to get him a printout of all the detailed voting statistics from the previous presidential election. He wanted to know who voted and why, where they voted, how each Farm voted, and what happened on each state's down ballot."

"Anything else?"

"Yes, keep an eye on the World Wide Web to see if the Farm is filtering any news about public opinion, politics, current memes, and anything else you think might be useful in our campaign. I'm going to schedule weekly Sunday morning planning meetings with you, Baxter, and my dad."

"Sounds good. You're making dinner." She pecked him on the cheek and got out of the cab.

On the ride home he wondered if he could video-in the senator without being detected. He'd let Baxter figure that out.

CHAPTER 28

SATURDAY NIGHT DOWNTOWN

The following Saturday noon, Sean, Eden, and Baxter got together at Eden's office. It was the first official meeting of the Sean Duncan election committee. The December weather was cool, the sky lightly overcast. A few people walked the mall, and fewer still ventured into the library. Eden had added a few Christmas decorations to her work-space—some holiday pictures, a potted plant with tinsel, but mostly the office space was filled with white boards, printers, boxes of paper, maps, a small refrigerator, and other things she thought should go in an election war room. Since her job was PR and advertising, no one said a word about her purchase requisitions.

"There's hardly room to walk around in here," Baxter said.

Eden looked at Baxter and smiled. "No, I won't say it."

"Yeah, I know. I need to go on a diet or go visit the Fat Man again."

"Don't do that unless you have to," Sean said. "You're too messed up when you get out of there."

"You too are plumping up again Mr. President." Baxter plopped down in a chair.

"It's hard not to. I'm a sucker for the IPAs and the cabernets. And of course, the steaks and chips and tacos and sausage and cheese."

Sean sat down, and Eden took her seat behind her desk.

"I've got all the election data you asked for." Eden pushed a mempod across the desk. "There's a lot there, but I asked it to arrange it in some semblance of importance. I hope it's okay."

"What is that thing?" Sean asked.

"It's a mempod, the latest in petabyte memory and data manipulation devices. Set your OED next to it. I told it to watch for you and download when it could."

"Cool," Sean said, setting his OED next to the pod until the download was complete. "Should be some exciting reading."

"What are we doing here?" Baxter asked. "Is there anything we can start? Any plans we can make? How about a written outline of tasks and deadlines? Is there anything to eat in that fridge?"

"No there isn't. That's your job Baxter." Eden smiled and nodded toward the door. "And bring some fresh fruit."

Hunger aside, Sean was having second thoughts. "Wait, Baxter, before you go, I want to say something. We all have jobs right now. Eden is doing her thing right here. You're still tech guru at the Welcome Center, and I'm on the hook for some fresh content for the Farm Channel." Sean paused and looked from Baxter to Eden. "Is a presidential campaign even doable? I don't want you guys to end up hating me for wasting your time. Please give it a lot of thought over the next week. If you're all in, then off we go. If not, then we hang it up. Also, please think about where you want to be after leaving this place. It's an important consideration." Sean got up and walked to the window. "But… for now I would like to propose that we get together this evening and go downtown for dinner. I'll buy. Eden, we'll pick you up at 6."

"How should I dress?" asked Baxter.

"Wear a tux."

Baxter dressed up a bit, but he didn't wear a tux. He wore his best sweat suit. No one dressed up at the Farms. Comfort was the norm and sweatpants stretched with the belly. The robocab dropped them off a block from downtown. Only shuttle buses were allowed on Corn Row, the name of the main drag.

"Sean, do you have an IOF card?" Baxter asked.

"What the hell is that?"

"I Owe Fat. It's for people with no bonus points but still want a restaurant meal. They pay it off in extra "fatributions.""

"Fatributions? No thanks. I have a cash card."

Theaters and restaurants lined both sides of the street. Saturday nights were busy in downtown Garcia. People who had earned bonuses for their "fatributions" came down to enjoy a night on the town; a restaurant meal and a movie perhaps. Restaurants were privately owned businesses and one had to pay for meals if one didn't have a bonus chit. Residents who had no credit but wanted to have fun on a Saturday night put their bill on an IOF card. Many residents went bankrupt. Their fatributions didn't cover their expenditures and were banned from further spending until they had caught up. Many died before they got caught up. The government reimbursed the businesses for their loss.

"What'll it be?" Sean asked. "Tex-Mex, Thai, Italian, Chinese, Hungarian, Cajun?"

"I'm okay with whatever you guys decide," said Eden.

"Let's do Chinese. They give you a lot for your money."

"I agree Baxter," Sean said. "But for a different reason. It seems they are the busiest from what I've seen so far. I'd like to be able to watch as many people as possible. Maybe even strike up a few conversations."

The restaurant was busy and the three had to wait fifteen minutes be seated. The decor was typical Chinese restaurant, but with heavy duty chairs. Most of the patrons were definitely Obies. There were some Rexics enjoying a night downtown as well. The restaurant had a full regular menu as well as an all-you-can-eat buffet. The buffet seemed to be very popular. Very large people carrying very large helpings formed an endless queue. While Sean and his friends waited, Sean witnessed several patrons who made a second trip in the short time they had to wait. For being so busy the place was quiet and one could hear the click of silverware on plates and the occasional slurp of soup. Most were too busy eating to talk.

A young Asian American girl led them to their table and passed out the menus.

"I'll be back in a few minutes to take your orders."

"Thank you," they all said practically in unison.

"I'm gonna go with the buffet," Baxter said.

"Chicken with Chinese vegetables for me." Eden folded her menu. "And I'll try the rice wine."

"Hunan pork, extra spicy. And some Chinese beer," Sean said. "And hot and sour soup."

"Yeah, beer for me too," Baxter added.

Baxter made two trips to the buffet while Sean and Eden enjoyed their meals. The food was decent and reasonably priced. During the meal Sean noticed Baxter spending a lot of time staring at the table next to them. Four young Obies, all women, sat there eating and enjoying themselves.

"Someone catch your eye Baxter?" Sean smiled.

Baxter blushed. "Actually yes. I was trying to screw up my courage and go introduce myself to the gal on the left."

Sean turned to look. "Good looking lady. Don't be shy. All she can say is get lost, but she just might give you her OED number."

The lady of interest got up to make another trip to the buffet. Baxter got up and managed to queue up behind her. Sean and Eden watched with interest and amusement as Baxter introduced himself. The woman smiled and offered her OED. Baxter scrambled to get his out of his pocket then held it up for the number transfer.

"Good job dude," Eden said as Baxter sat down. "What's her name?"

"Rosetta Stone. I think it's a fake, but she did give me her number."

Sean paid the bill and the group stepped out into the cool evening air. The sidewalks were busy with Obies shuffling along and Rexics stepping around them. Sean found it interesting that there was no police presence, but realized there were cameras on every street corner and building. He knew from his research that crime was rare on the farms. No one had any need to steal and mental illness was diagnosed and handled quickly.

Sean approached two women who were window shopping at a clothing boutique. He waved for Eden and Baxter to join him. "Excuse me ladies. I'm Sean Duncan from the Farm News Network. Would you mind answering a few questions? Nothing personal, just how you might be voting in next year's presidential election and why."

The two looked at each other and giggled. They were big and their bodies jiggled when they giggled. "Will we be on TV?" the larger one asked.

"I might be able to make that happen. Baxter can you please record this? Thanks." Baxter pulled out his OED and began to record.

"Can I get your names? Just your first names. We won't use them if you don't want us to. Also, how long you've been at Central Iowa Farm."

"I'm Tina. Ten years."

"And I'm Wanda. We came together so it's ten years for me too."

"I know it's early, but I wonder if you've given any thought to next year's presidential election. What kind of things you'd like to see in a candidate, for example. Any thoughts on that?"

"Oh honey," Tina laughed. "You're dreaming. I don't think about that shit until voting day! I don't care who's running as long as they support the farms. We're enjoying it here. Right Wanda?"

"Got that right. I only vote because it's the law, and to get a discount on my Christmas shopping. Last year I wrote in Mickey Mouse. I read where Mickey Mouse got a half million votes."

The three walked a block off Corn Row and Sean called for a cab. Baxter did a quick disconnect of the on-board voice recorder.

"Wow, that was strange, but about what I expected," Baxter said.

"Interesting voters, those two," Sean said. "Garcia was

ensuring the survival of his Farm System when he made voting mandatory for farm residents. I wonder if it was his idea to get the big etailers to give "I voted" discounts."

"I read somewhere the Chinese did it first," Baxter said. "But I'm not sure."

"It also helped boost country wide turnout when he declared presidential election day a national holiday," Sean said.

"That was Garcia?" Baxter asked.

"Yes. My dad thought that was one of his few good ideas." Sean turned to Eden. "What did you think of those two?"

"I don't think we're going to win the farm vote," Eden said.

The robocab pulled into Sean's apartment lot.

"Are you ready to go home?" he asked Eden.

"I'd rather not." Eden gave him a look.

"God I'm dense. Come on in Eden. Baxter, we'll talk tomorrow. Have a good night."

"You two do the same."

CHAPTER 29

VOTING DAY USA

In addition to making voting day a national holiday, President Garcia also introduced additional election changes that were far more controversial. By 2040 everyone in the country had access to high-speed fiber optic internet. It was then that the government began developing a hack-proof system of online voting. The goal was to increase voter turnout from the dismal 30% or so that had become the norm. The idealists thought that 100% turnout was possible. The pragmatists were hoping for 50%. The system used an excellent facial recognition system developed by the Chinese and improved over time by NASA. Stored images were able to age with the passage of years. Someone who hadn't voted in a decade was still recognized and a new image was subsequently stored. There were other security checks in place based on IRS, medical, and public records. Anyone caught voting as someone other than themselves faced a very public execution.

"Do you remember the Tommy Hatfield trial?" Sean rolled on his side to face Eden.

They were lying in bed enjoying a post-coital moment.

"Wasn't he the guy that got hanged for voting twice?"

"Yeah. Did you watch the hanging?"

"No. Did you?"

"Yes I did."

"Oh Sean, that's disgusting."

"Yes it was. I threw up afterward." Sean swung his legs out of bed. "But it sure put an end to voter fraud."

Sean showered, dressed, and started breakfast while Eden got her shower.

They were enjoying another cup of coffee after some oatmeal and toast.

"I hadn't given any thought to a write-in campaign," Sean said. "I wonder if we would still have to register with the election commission."

"I'll look into it Monday," Eden said. "Although I'm not sure that's the way to go. On the other hand, registering as a new political party amounts to the same thing in a way."

"You're probably right. Having a registered party name and a professional logo may get us some of the Mickey Mouse votes."

Eden got out her OED and asked it "How many votes did Mickey Mouse receive in the last presidential election?" She read the answer. "Six hundred and twenty-seven thousand, give or take a few. Not bad for a fictional rodent."

"I bet most came from the Farms," Sean said.

"That information is probably buried somewhere in all that election data I gave you." Eden replied.

"I'll be digging into that tomorrow. Maybe it'll give me some insight. On another subject do you have any thoughts on who we should interview for our first man-on-the-street segment?"

"Not really."

"I'm thinking that when the weather gets decent, we

should stand outside a church and flag a few folks as they're coming out of their service. They should be in a giving mood, I would think."

"We'll need press badges."

"I don't think the Farm Channel issues them. We'll just have to wing it."

CHAPTER 30

MAN ON THE STREET

Most of the Central Iowa Farm churches were Protestant with a few Catholic churches, one Synagogue, and one Mosque. Attendees were almost all Rexics, since the Obies were disinclined to make the effort. Getting up early on a Sunday was hard for a lot of them, especially the drinkers, which many were. Some churches began offering services on Sunday afternoons, but they were poorly attended and soon ended.

"Would you like to attend a service? Were you a churchgoer in your previous life?" Sean asked Eden as the two made their way to the street. This winter day was mild and bright due to the light permacloud layer. Brutal Iowa winters were a thing of the past. There was no snow on the ground.

"When I was growing up. My parents were moderately serious Lutherans and we attended church most Sundays. I haven't been in years and don't have any desire to attend today. How about you?"

"Not hardly. I was raised Catholic and like many Catholics I evolved into an agnostic. Too much bullshit for me. My parents continued to attend Mass until my mother died. In the eyes of the church what my father did was a mortal sin, but I doubt if he believed in sin, heaven, or hell, after watching my mom suffer." Sean stopped and asked his OED where the nearest Lutheran church was. It was only a mile and half away.

"An easy walk on this beautiful Sunday morning."

Sean and Eden arrived at the church at 10:30. The church information sign said that services began at 10, so that they had about a half hour wait before the believers were let out. They sat on a bench situated near the church steps and discussed what questions they should ask besides the usual: what's your name, how long have you been at Central Iowa, what do you do, how do you like it, etc. They thought they should ease into politics if the conversation offered them an easy segue.

The grounds around the church were spotless and the church was well maintained. At 11:00 the doors opened, and the parishioners began to file out. No one seemed to be in a hurry. People stopped to chat with friends and neighbors, enjoying the pleasant day. Sean and Eden got up and approached two older couples who were having a discussion on the church-front concrete apron.

"Pardon us, folks. I'm Sean and this is Eden. We're from the Farm Channel Television Network. Could we have a moment of your time to ask you a few questions?"

One of the white-haired gentlemen, who looked to be about 75 years old, stared at Sean for a moment. "I know you. You're Senator Duncan's kid. You appear in the Farm propaganda ads. I wouldn't give you the time of day young man. Your father would be spinning in his grave if he knew what you were doing."

"Did you vote for my father?"

"Damn right I did. He had the common sense to realize what an abomination these Farms would be."

The woman next to him put her hand on his arm. "Now Jim, don't be getting all worked up."

"There's more to that than meets the eye," Sean said. "But I'm curious sir. If you feel the Farms are an abomination, why are you here?"

"My family had a farm here since the late 1800s. The government forced me to sell it to them. They let us keep our house and a couple of acres. That's why the hell I'm here."

"I'm sorry about your family farm and I certainly don't agree with what happened. My doing promos for the Farms was pretty much against my will but it allowed me to find out the truth about what happened to my father. I can't go into that now, but I will tell you that I was part of the resistance and I… never mind. Do you have a minute to talk? Jim, is it?"

"Yup. This is my wife Jenny. I'll give you a minute. Hang on." Jim and Jenny said goodbye to their friends.

"Let's go sit down." Sean led them to the bench. Eden sat next to Jenny and Sean next to Jim. "How many other farms were forced to sell? Do you have any idea?"

"Hundreds. Not all families hung around. Many did. We got enough money to retire comfortably, but it still didn't make up for losing our land."

"What would you like to see done with the Farms?"

"Shut 'em down and send all the fatsos home. Or let 'em stay 'til they croak. Give the farmers their land back. But it ain't going to happen. Been too long embedded, too much diesel fuel riding on the Obie contributions."

"Do you still vote?"

"I haven't voted since the last candidate promised to

dismantle the Farm system. And that's been years. There's so many people living on all the Farms now that they swing the vote to the pro-Farm candidates. Now there aren't any anti-Farm candidates left."

"Aren't you required to vote?"

"Nope. Our property remains private, like the other farmers. Technically separate from the farm."

"So, tearing down the Farms and returning the land to the original owners would be your top priorities in next year's presidential election?"

"Yup, but I don't expect any candidate to run on that platform."

"You might be surprised," Sean said. "Thanks for your time Jim."

Jim gave Sean a long look before he said goodbye, stood, put his hand out to Jenny, and the two walked away.

Sean and Eden sat in silence for a moment. "Damn. I wish Baxter was here to record that. It would have made for a good campaign ad. What did Jenny have to say?" Sean asked. They got up and started back to Sean's place.

"She was nice. She said Jim gets riled anytime the Farms are mentioned. He hasn't gotten over it. They had been mid-American conservatives all their lives, but when the choice was voting for a liberal who was against the proposed Farm system or a conservative who was going to confiscate our property and destroy the only life we've ever known, the choice was simple. She does like being retired though. What did Jim have to say?"

"Well, he's one vote we'll get for sure. Said shutting down the Farms and getting his land back are his priorities."

"I suspect he won't live to see it."

CHAPTER 31

EDEN'S REVEAL

On the way back to Sean's apartment, he and Eden took the long way around to stop at a Freeburger to order vanilla shakes. They sat at one of the concrete tables.

Eden took a sip and said, "I never asked you. Are you married?"

Sean spread his left hand on the table.

"That doesn't mean anything. You know that."

"I am not married. I was married. It didn't work out. We had differences that couldn't be reconciled."

"What happened? If you don't mind me asking."

"We disagreed on the Farms. She thought it made sense. It caught me by surprise. I never saw that side of her. We had many heated arguments about it. One night she blurted out that she was going to sign up when enrollment opened. I filed for divorce the next day."

"Wow. That had to be tough. Where did she end up?"

"Northern California Farm. I never heard from her." Sean stirred the shake with his straw. "And I never wanted to. I'm just glad we never had kids."

"When did all this happen?"

"Just after my father was convicted and sent to prison.

I suspect she reported me to the Obesity Police at some point. But enough about me. Your turn," Sean said. "Were you ever married? Any kids?"

Eden stared into her shake. She blinked a tear out of her eye. "I almost got married."

Sean waited. "And?"

"And like you, we had differences of opinion. Although not about the farms." Eden wiped her nose with a Freeburger napkin. "I wanted children and he didn't. Of course my parents wanted grandchildren. When I realized I couldn't change his mind, I canceled the wedding… two days before it was supposed to happen. What a clusterfuck."

"I admire your courage. That couldn't have been easy. Good for you. Do you still want to have kids?"

Eden looked up from her shake and looked at Sean. "Do you?"

"I haven't thought about it in years. I always thought it would be kind of neat to be a dad. I think I would have been a good one."

"You still can."

"Hmm?"

"I'm pregnant."

Sean sat staring at Eden for a long minute. "Really?"

"Yes, really. About two months along."

"And it's my kid?"

"Jesus Sean! I haven't been boffing Baxter. Of course it's your kid. And now we have a decision to make."

"Decision?"

Eden looked at Sean with a slight smile and shook her head. "I would think that with your background, intelligence, common sense, and kindness you would have a better grasp of what I'm telling you. We either keep it or we don't. I'm not making this decision alone."

"I'm sorry. Just give me a second to process this. It's a shock for sure." Sean stared at Eden and a smile slowly grew on his face. "I'm going to be a father. I don't believe it. Wait'll I tell my dad."

"So that's a vote for being more than a sperm donor?"

"Oh hell yes."

"I'm glad you're on board. I couldn't abort him… her. And I wanted her… him to have a father in her life. You'll be a good father."

"Should we get married?"

"Good question. He'll have your last name if that's what you're worried about. I'll see to it."

"I don't think I'd want a Farm wedding. What do you think?" Sean got up and tossed their shake cups into the trash.

"Not only do I not want a Farm wedding, but I also don't want our baby born here."

"Why not? The Farms make a pretty big deal out of babies and their parents. Free formula, free diapers, … and free delivery. No medical bills."

"Something to consider I guess," Eden said. "We have time to think about it."

Back at the apartment the couple spent hours thinking and arguing about names, while college basketball played without sound on the ultradef.

CHAPTER 32

BAXTER'S FIRST DATE

A week later, Baxter went to the city of Garcia and found Rosetta's building, Building 30, with no issues. Indeed, Baxter had called Rosetta when he had left Sean and Eden the previous week. They talked for a bit on their OEDs then switched over to their Cackle accounts and talked face to face. One of the first things Baxter learned was that Rosetta Stone was her real name and that her parents evidently had a sense of humor. Rosetta didn't care to talk over Cackle, so they made a date for the following weekend.

Baxter took the elevator to the second floor and found apartment 30-211. The door opened before he could knock. "C'mon in Mr. Bodecker." To his surprise she gave him a long hug. He hadn't been hugged since his mother dropped him off in front of his dorm on his first day of college.

Baxter followed her into the apartment, which didn't look different from every other one he'd been in. At least it made finding the bathroom easy. "Would you like a drink?" Rosetta asked.

Baxter found himself not knowing how to respond, think,

or act. This was the first date of his life, and he was struggling. "Sure, if you wouldn't mind or if you want one too."

"What would you like?"

"I'll have what you're having."

"Baxter, relax, you wouldn't like what I'm having. I like foo-foo drinks. You look like a beer guy."

"I'm not very good at this. I'm pretty nervous."

"Well don't be. I don't bite and I like you. So sit your fat ass down and I'll bring you a beer. Glass?"

"Yes, please."

While she prepared their drinks, Baxter watched her. Rosetta was an Obie, but not sloppy. Big boned and tall, she was Rubenesque with smooth dark skin. She wore a dashiki and sweatpants that didn't hide any of her curves. She wore her hair in a retro-cornrow style which was the first thing that had caught Baxter's eye at the Chinese restaurant. If Baxter could have expressed what he'd felt then, it would have been "love at first sight".

"What's a foo-foo drink?" Baxter asked as Rosetta handed him his beer.

"Sweet shit. I'm having a Rosetta Bushwhacker—chocolate milk shake and pina colada. Here, have a sip."

Baxter took a sip. "Yeah… foo-foo is a good term for that. That's a whole dessert." Baxter took a swig of his beer to rinse out the taste. "Where would you like to go for dinner?"

Rosetta sipped her drink. "Hmm… I think I want to make you dinner and stay right here. What would you like to eat?"

"Really? I said I'd treat."

"It ain't about the money honey. The food here comes with the apartment. The powers that be keep hoping I get fat enough to require a suctioning. Not happening. Anyway, I just don't feel like going out. Do you mind?"

Baxter's mind was racing. He'd like nothing better than to stay right where he was and look at this beautiful woman. He was hoping for possibilities that he felt were probably out of the question. "No, I don't mind at all. What's for dinner?" Baxter's response had surprised him. He had wanted to say "Whatever you want."

"I thought I'd bake some lasagna, make a salad and serve it with some fine red wine and crusty bread. That good?"

Baxter stood up and looked around.

"What are you doing?" Rosetta asked.

"I wanted to see if I was in Seventh Heaven."

Dinner was relaxed and the food delicious. Baxter did his best to eat slowly and only finished a little before Rosetta. She cleaned the table, put the dishes in the dishwasher and poured them each a generous glass of wine. They retired to the sofa with some soft music playing from a station on the ultradef. A fireplace screensaver was the video. In ultradef it was very realistic.

"So have you visited the Fat Man?" Baxter asked.

"Never have, never will. I pay my Fat Tax every year on time and without complaint. How about you?"

"Once, but I'm approaching another trip soon unless I quit eating so much. Not a good time at all. Hurts like hell when the drugs wear off and then you're sore for a week. I never asked how you ended up at Central Iowa Farm. Why are you here?"

Rosetta smiled. "I studied nursing in college and got a job at a hospital in Omaha. After Central Iowa was in business for a decade or so, they realized they had a health crisis and a nursing shortage. They were offering a lot more money than I was making so I took a job at Garcia General. Been there ever since."

"What kind of health crisis?"

"Heart disease and strokes, type 2 diabetes, certain cancers, digestive problems, sleep apnea, osteoarthritis; all diseases obesity related. People here linger in very poor health for a long time before they go into the energy stream. We really don't go to extreme measures to keep them alive, but we do try to keep them comfortable until the end." Rosetta sipped her wine. "It's quite sad really."

"How do you deal with it? Sounds depressing."

"It is. I just don't get close to anyone and try to see them as the government does—just a source of energy." Rosetta got up and sat down next to Baxter. "Tell me what you do."

Baxter felt her closeness and a stirring below his belt. He tried thinking about the dust bunnies under his bench at the Tracking Lab. "I got behind on my taxes. Couldn't pay so I was sent to Central Iowa to get caught up. I have a degree in electronics and got a job in the Tracking Lab. I kind of liked it here until I met a friend who convinced me that I didn't really want to spend the rest of my life growing fat for the government. After hearing your story about the illness, I want to get slimmer and stay healthy. I have a sister who would like me out of here too. You got family nearby?"

"Mom and dad are gone. One brother in the service— Navy. Haven't seen him in years. But I have some good friends and we have fun. I was with them last week at the restaurant and they all got a kick out of you ogling me. One of them was hoping she could get your number. You're a good-looking guy Baxter."

"No shit? I hope I picked the right one."

"You did." Rosetta turned and kissed him.

"I've never done this," Baxter croaked.

"I'm gonna teach you tonight."

CHAPTER 33

REVEREND THOMAS

Baxter got up early and managed to leave without waking Rosetta, who was still snoring. He relived the entire evening several times on his drive home, grinning like an idiot each time. He showered and changed before heading for Sean's place to see if there was a campaign meeting going on.

Baxter knocked. "You all decent?"

"Come on in Baxter."

"Good morning Sean. Good morning Eden. How are you guys this fine morning? Can I get a coffee and muffin?"

"You're in a good mood this morning Baxter." Eden said as she poured him a cup. She looked at Sean who was smiling and looking at her. She turned back to Baxter. "Did you see Rosetta last night?"

"I did." Baxter could not stop smiling.

"And did you…" Eden said.

"Yes he did," Sean interjected. "Good for you. Judging from your mood, things went well."

"No comment, but I think I'm in love."

Sean shook his hand and Eden gave him a hug. "I hope

you were more careful than we were," Eden said. "I'm pregnant."

"She's a nurse so… wait, what?"

"We're having a baby—in about 7 months."

"Holy shit! That's great. At least I hope it's great," Baxter said.

"It is. I'm looking forward to being a father."

"My turn." Baxter hugged Eden and shook Sean's hand. "If it's a boy you should name him Baxter."

"And if it's a girl, Baxta?"

"Um… probably not. So, what's the plan today?"

Eden retrieved a muffin from the refrigerator and put it in the microwave to warm. The three sat around the dining table.

"I'd like to make a first cut of our new campaign ad," Sean said. "At least decide on what it should say and what video we use."

"Isn't it kind of early? We won't be airing it for nearly a year. Things might change by then," Eden said. "Also, didn't you say your father wanted to help? We should seek his input, I think."

Sean leaned back in his chair. "I suppose you're right. I wonder if we could get up to see him today? I want you to meet him soon anyway."

"Is the President's Suite open on Sundays?" Baxter asked.

"Ask your OED."

Baxter did. "Since it's before Memorial Day, tours only happen during the week. Can you get us in Sean?"

"I'll need to get some kind of pass from Garcia. I'll do that tomorrow. Meanwhile, I think we need to go back and talk to our friends from church, Jim and Jenny."

"Who?" Baxter asked.

"Last Sunday Eden and I stood outside a church and flagged an older couple to ask them a few questions in hopes of getting some material for our man-on-the-street segments that we want to do for the Farm Channel. Turns out they hate the Farms due to the government taking their farm and leaving them a few acres and a bunch of money. I wish we had recorded the conversation. But we can see if they're at church today and if they'd be willing to go on the record. What do you think, Eden?"

"Sure. It's nice enough to walk to church again."

"Walk?" Baxter said. "How far is it?"

"Baxter, you're going to need to increase your stamina. I'm sure Rosetta will want more next time. A walk is a good start."

They headed out in the cool late January morning with the smell of freshly turned earth in the air. Tractors roared in nearby fields. Fertilizer trucks rumbled by. Due to climate change, the farm fields were prepped early in the year. It was a busy time at the Farms. The three arrived at the church just as the congregation was getting out. They stood near the steps looking for Jim and Jenny. Neither Sean nor Eden spotted them. As the last parishioners were shaking hands with the reverend at the church door, Sean said, "Let's go talk to the minister and ask him about his flock."

The minister was about to close the door and go in when Sean waved to him. He stopped to greet the trio. Eden grabbed Sean's arm and said "Hold it. That's the guy from my parent's fake funeral. He won't want to talk to me, and I don't want to talk to him."

"He probably won't recognize you since he must do hundreds of funerals a year. Besides, he might appreciate an apology for the black eye." Sean put his arm around her and urged her forward. "I'll do the talking."

"Good morning reverend. I'm Sean Duncan from the Farm Channel TV network. How are you this morning?"

"I'm fine, thank you," the reverend said, extending his hand. "I'm Reverend Thomas."

"This is Baxter Bodecker and Eden Sprayberry."

"I know Ms. Sprayberry." The reverend shook Baxter's hand.

"I'd like to apologize for my outburst in the funeral chapel. I was very upset. Please forgive me." Eden stuck out her hand and the reverend took it in his hands.

"I have forgiven you. But I want you to know that I'm not told ahead of time if the relatives are aware that the deceased are replicas. I assumed you knew until you asked to touch them. I've since inquired before every funeral service. So—how can I be of service this morning?"

"We came looking for a couple of your parishioners we met here last Sunday—a Jim and Jenny. Older couple, retired farmers. Since we didn't see them, I thought we'd interview you. If you don't mind, of course."

"What is the purpose of the interview? I'm not a very interesting person."

"We're trying to do some human-interest stories to spice up the Farm Channel if you would. I thought a feature on the Central Iowa Farm churches may be a place to start. Just some background, the makeup of your flock, and anything else you'd like to add."

"When will your piece air?"

"We just got started, so I'm not sure. I'll certainly let you know so you don't miss it. Can we go inside? I'd like to get some shots of you by the altar."

"By all means." The reverend showed them in.

"I'll get some shots out here after we're finished inside," Baxter said.

The inside of the church was classic Christian—a row of pews on either side of the main aisle, the altar on a slightly raised platform, stained glass windows, and a choir loft. It was quiet as they walked slowly to the altar. Baxter had Reverend Thomas stand in various poses around the altar as he recorded.

"Are you married? Children?" asked Sean.

"Yes. I have a son, 26, and a daughter, 24."

"Do they live around here?"

"No, they both attended college in California then got jobs there – son in LA, daughter in San Francisco. My wife and I are empty nesters now."

"So how has this church been in existence," asked Sean.

"It was started in the 1880s by German immigrants. This building was constructed in the 1940s."

"So are most of the parishioners still of German descent?"

"I'd say so. I know Jim and Jenny Schneider are."

"What would you say the general feeling is regarding the Farms and Farm System?"

"Many lost their farms to the government. There is still a lot of resentment."

"How do you feel about them? I know you provide services to them."

"I do. It helps provide a living. Most of my parishioners are retired on Social Security. Not much in the collection plate most Sundays. So, I guess I'm neutral, but I wouldn't mind if they were shut down. From what I see there is a lot of gluttony, lust, and idolatry because of them."

"Do you pay the fat tax?"

"Churches and clerics are exempt."

"Ah yes. Of course." Sean took a long look around. "Reverend Thomas, thanks so much for your time. We'll take a few pictures outside and be on our way."

Reverend Thomas pulled a business card out of a pocket. "Here, take my information. I want to know when this will be aired. I hope I don't catch hell for being honest about how I feel about the farms."

Sean and Eden waited while Baxter walked around the old church getting footage and stills. He especially liked the steeple and spire and took several angles of them. "Who's the keeper of the video?" Baxter asked.

"Eden. I'm not organized enough," Sean replied.

"I don't mind. Send them to my library account. Part of my public relations degree was studying video editing. I enjoyed it and aced the course. I'll write up the voiceover script. Baxter, your baritone is perfect for narration. The problem as I see it is that we'll only get about 10 minutes of content out of today's effort."

"We'll just need to do a couple more interviews and we got a half hour segment. Who should we talk to next?" Sean looked at Eden then Baxter. Eden looked at Baxter.

"Rosetta," Sean and Eden said simultaneously.

"Rosetta?" Baxter asked. "Why her?"

"You happened to mention she was a nurse. That's definitely a different perspective than a man of the cloth. Please tell her it's a chance to be on TV and we won't embarrass her. She might like the opportunity," Sean said.

Baxter scratched his head and smiled. "She'll probably love it."

CHAPTER 34

ROSETTA STONE

After the interview with Reverand Thomas, Baxter called Rosetta and made a date for the following Friday. He asked if she would like to have dinner at the Chinese restaurant where they first met, and she said it was a great idea. He hadn't said anything about a possible interview, waiting until he thought the moment was right. Maybe the moment would be right when they were in bed—after she had an orgasm. He wasn't sure if he could tell.

The evening went well. Rosetta was in a good mood as was Baxter. After dinner Baxter suggested she come back to his place, just to see where he lived and to spend the night if she wanted. She wanted.

They made out in the back seat of the robocab all the way to Baxter's apartment.

"Well, this is where I live. Pretty much like the place where you live, except nowhere near as nicely decorated," Baxter said. "What would you like to drink?"

"You got any foo foo drinks?" Rosetta laughed. "Just kidding. Some red wine would be nice."

"Coming up."

After a bottle of a French Bordeaux and even better sex than they had the first time, Baxter felt a confidence that he'd never experienced before. "I feel really good," he said. "I hope you do too."

Rosetta rolled toward him and put her arm across his chest. "You're learning, baby. I feel great."

"I'm glad. You're a good teacher." Baxter turned toward her. "I have a friend that is trying to come up with some human-interest stories for a series he's proposed for the Farm Channel Network. We did an interview last Sunday with a preacher. Now he wants to interview you. I think you'd be great. What do you think?"

"I'd be on TV?"

"Absolutely."

"I'm all in."

The following morning Baxter contacted Sean and Eden to set up an interview with Rosetta. Due to her schedule Rosetta was only available on Tuesdays, so Tuesday it was. They met at Eden's library office.

"So good to meet you," Eden said, giving Rosetta a hug. "Baxter has good taste."

"That's not the only thing he's got that's good," Rosetta winked at Eden.

"Oh man," Baxter smiled at the ceiling.

"Thanks so much for coming today," Sean said. "We really appreciate it. Baxter will be recording the interview, while Eden and I ask questions. Feel free to expand on any subject or bring up something we might miss. First, a question you probably get a lot—why did your parents name you Rosetta?"

Rosetta laughed. "They both had a weird sense of humor, or maybe they wanted me to be bilingual. I didn't think anything of it until one of my junior high English teachers sent our class a Wiki-link to the Rosetta Stone from Egypt, which I had never heard of. At first I was embarrassed, but now I love it. I think it's pretty."

"I do too," Eden said. "Baxter, are you ready to record?"

"Yeah, but just a second."

"Baxter filled us in a little about your background, but if you don't mind, why don't you tell us what you do and how you ended up at Central Iowa. That way we'll have it in your own words for the TV segment."

"I'm really going to be on TV?"

"Eventually, yes. We don't have a date yet, since you are only our second interview. We have one done and need one more after this to fill in a half hour segment."

"OK, I'm ready," said Baxter, and the interview began.

Rosetta did a good job telling her story for the camera. Baxter flitted around, getting her from every angle. When she was finished Sean asked her, "So do you vote?"

"Hell yes I vote. My parents were firm believers in our democracy and insisted I vote. They didn't tell me how to vote, even though they made their liberal views very clear. I've never missed an election."

"I'm not sure you're old enough, but do you have any recollection of the Garcia versus Duncan elections?"

"Vaguely. Just the second one, I think. I remember my folks being upset when Garcia won again. Why do you ask?"

"I'm Senator Duncan's son."

"Really? Oh yeah... I remember you now from the Farm ads. You're famous."

"Hardly. More like infamous. Have you ever been in the Garcia library before?"

"No, but I've been meaning to."

"Eden, would you be so kind as to give Rosetta a quick

tour?" Sean asked, then turned to Eden and mouthed the word 'please'.

"C'mon Rosetta. Let me show you around." Eden led her out the door. Baxter was about to follow when Sean held up his hand to stop him.

"I wanted to talk to you alone for a minute. I know you're in love and all that, but what is your feeling about Rosetta's ability to keep a secret? What have you told her already?"

"I haven't said anything about you running for president. Didn't even tell her who your father is. I haven't known her long enough to get a feel for her politics, although she does pay all her Fat Tax."

Sean got up and stared out the window. "I hate to ask, but would do a background check on her. As best you can anyway."

"Sure. She's probably done one on me by now."

"Thanks."

Eden and Rosetta returned in an hour acting like they'd been best friends for years. Sean thought this a good sign. He knew Baxter would be hopelessly lovestruck for months and didn't want to lose Baxter's efforts in the coming campaign. By letting Rosetta into the small inner circle he'd be guaranteeing Baxter's continued support. He just needed to see where she stood politically, as well as her true feelings about the Farms.

"Where's a restroom?" Rosetta asked.

"Down the hall to the left," Eden answered.

"I'll go with you. And use the one on the right," Baxter said.

While Rosetta and Baxter were gone, Sean asked Eden about her impressions.

"I like her. She's upbeat and curious. She enjoyed see-ing the two election halls and asked questions I couldn't answer."

"Did you get a feeling about her attitude towards the Farms?"

"I think she's neutral—happy to be employed at Garcia General, but only because they pay well and take care of patients well. No bitching. Apolitical I think."

"Well, I don't want Baxter blabbing in a moment of pas-sion and her thinking we were keeping a secret. I'm going to suggest we all go meet my father. Which means I'll have to tell him."

"Really? That's wonderful. I've been dying to meet him."

CHAPTER 35

SENATOR DUNCAN HAS COMPANY

After Baxter and Rosetta returned to Eden's office, Sean said, "Rosetta, I have something I want to share with you since Baxter may talk in his sleep and you'd find out anyway. You must promise not to share it with anyone. It'll be out there soon, but the timing is critical to what we're planning."

Rosetta looked from Sean to Baxter to Eden. "You guys planning a heist or something? Sounds ominous. But I can keep a secret... as long as it doesn't involve a murder or something like that."

"Nothing illegal, except me reneging on a non-disclosure agreement, which I'm not sure would stand up in court anyway." Sean got up and closed the office door. "When Eden gave you the tour did she show you the presidential suite on the top floor?"

"I've never been up there myself," Eden said. "But we didn't go."

"We'll be going up there shortly." Sean paused. "To visit my dad."

"Your father is alive and lives here?" Rosetta said in a loud whisper.

"He does." Sean gave her a brief rundown on how he came to discover a connection between his father and the Garcia Library and later to discover that his father was alive and living in an apartment right above them.

Rosetta looked at Baxter. "You keep secrets pretty well Mr. Bodecker."

"I had other things on my mind during our brief encounters, Ms. Stone."

"That's not all of it," Sean said. "I'm also going to run for president."

"Holy Crap. This gets more interesting by the minute. If I can help, let me know. I could use a new adventure."

"Thanks. I need all the help I can get." Sean walked to the door. "When we get upstairs act like tourists while I let my father know we're here. Then, when the guard is distracted, which she usually is, we can pop in."

The four rode the elevator to the penthouse. Sean woke up the guard and showed her his pass. Eden and Rosetta, never having seen the place before, had no trouble behaving as tourists.

"Well, this is something, ain't it?" Rosetta said to Eden.

"Yeah, no kidding. Makes me want to be first lady."

Sean walked to his father's suite and let himself in. Soon, the door opened, and Sean caught Eden's eye and waved them over. The guard had her head down and was sound asleep. They stepped in to meet Senator Duncan.

Sean did the introductions. "Dad, this is the lady I mentioned, Eden Sprayberry."

"I'm so glad to meet you, Eden." He gave her a hug.

"And this is Rosetta Stone."

"Rosetta Stone, what a lovely name." He gave her a hug too.

"And this is my good friend, Baxter Bodecker."

The senator shook Baxter's hand firmly. "Very pleased to meet you, Baxter. Well, I must say, it is quite a new experience for me having this many people in my apartment. Please make yourselves comfortable. Would anyone like something to drink?"

"We can't stay long dad," Sean said. "I think I violated the terms of my NDA by bringing my team up, but I don't care. I wanted them to meet you. I hope you're not upset."

"Not at all. I've been a semi-hermit too long. Sean, did you get the essays I sent?"

"I did dad, but haven't had a chance to read them yet. But I will."

Sean filled his father in on the Farm Channel gig and asked him if he would agree to an interview. "It's time you came out of the closet, dad. At least give it some thought. You said you wanted to help my campaign. This would be a start."

"I don't know, son. The powers that be may get upset."

"And what would they do? Throw an 82-year-old former senator in jail?"

Eden raised her hand.

"What? Are we in grade school?" Rosetta asked.

"Sean, are you going to tell your dad?"

Sean looked at Eden with a puzzled expression. Then it dawned on him. "Dad, you're going to be a grandfather."

The senator's expression didn't change for a bit. Then, a soft smile and a tear appeared. "I'm…overcome a little. It's something I've always imagined. When are you due Eden?"

"Next September. If it's a boy we're naming it Darius."

"We are?" Sean replied.

"What was your wife's name, Senator Duncan?" Eden asked.

"Laura."

"And if it's a girl, we'll name her Laura," Eden said.

Sean looked at Eden and then his father. Then he began to tear up.

"Man, I think I'm an extra in a soap opera," Rosetta said as she wiped her eyes with a tissue.

"What's a soap opera?" Baxter asked.

"Baxter, you are so clueless."

The senator got up and shook his son's hand, then leaned over and kissed Eden on the cheek. "It's been a long time since I've been this happy. And yes, I'll do a campaign ad for you. Just give me a script so I can practice before it gets recorded."

CHAPTER 36

SPOTLIGHT ON WILL

Back in Eden's office Sean and Baxter finished Rosetta's interview and video for the TV segment. Rosetta was warm and animated, answering questions in detail. Sean thought she would be perfect in the campaign ads they were planning.

"All done?" Baxter asked. "If so, I'll pack up the set."

"We still need one more interview," Sean said.

"How about Director Hawley," Baxter suggested.

"Good idea, but he's on the Farm Channel too much already," Sean replied. "But it does give me an idea. The old man, Will, the custodian who works in the Welcome Center basement is an interesting character. He's been here since the get go. He'd be a good one. Let's pay him a visit tomorrow, Baxter. Bring your gear."

The following morning, Sean and Baxter rode together to the Welcome Center. They were careful not to discuss their planned interview with Will.

"I hope he's in today," Sean said as they made their way to the basement. "He said he's part time."

"He should be in. I called Operations yesterday afternoon

and said I needed to update the custodian's computer and give him a quick lesson on a few new features. They said they'd ask him to come in."

"Very good, Baxter."

They found Will at his desk reading a well worn paperback. "Good morning, Will," Sean said. "How have you been?"

Will got up and shook Sean's hand and reached to shake Baxter's. "Hi there. I'm Will."

"Baxter Bodecker. Pleased to meet you."

"Ops said you're going to make some changes to my computer? I rarely use the damn thing."

"Well, the updates won't take long. It'll bring yours up to the same level as Ops."

"No problem. As long as I don't have to read a new manual."

"You won't. In fact, you won't notice any difference at all." Baxter smiled and sat down at the computer.

"Speaking of reading," Sean said, "what are you reading?"

"It's an old biography of Abraham Lincoln. Found it at a garage sale one day when I was out for a walk."

"People still have garage sales?" Baxter asked.

"Sure, but you need to get out and about on a weekend."

"Will, I wonder if I could interview you for a new series I'm putting together for the Farm Channel?"

"Interview me? Who'd want to see and listen to me?"

"A lot of people. You've been here since the beginning, and I believe it would be of interest to many. We're not talking about anything too long. Probably a 10 minute segment which would be one of three segments in my first half hour long show. I've interviewed a Lutheran Minister and a nurse from Garcia General so far."

"Why are you doing this?"

"Have you watched the Farm Channel lately? It's boring as hell. We're just trying to liven it up."

"The last time you were here you asked if I'd seen your father. I said not recently. Have you seen your father recently?"

Sean's face registered his surprise at the question. He hesitated a moment then said, "Yes I have. Just yesterday as a matter of fact. How did you know to ask me that?"

"I just thought you would eventually find him."

"So you knew he was still alive?"

"There's a few of us at Central Iowa that know. It's sort of like a secret club. We don't talk about it. How's he doing?"

"Pretty good. He agreed to do a campaign ad for me. I'm running for president. You can tell your club, but don't talk about it."

Will gave Sean a hug. "I'll vote for you. And I'll do your interview. You about done with your bullshit Baxter?"

"All done, sir." Baxter got up and pulled a small lamp out of his backpack. "Do we need the bedsheet I brought?"

"I don't think so. Will, sitting at his desk, will be fine," Sean said.

Will talked for an hour about his life and his time at the Farm while Baxter recorded and Sean asked the occasional question.

"Will, that was great. In fact, I think I'm going to feature you in your own half-hour segment. Of course, I'll let you review it prior to the broadcast. Sound good?"

"You'll be making the Farm Channel more boring, I'm thinking," Will said.

"Not hardly," Baxter said, "I was fascinated. Thanks for sharing, Will."

"I enjoyed it. Also, I'm not sure Senator Duncan will remember me, I only met him once, and that was just briefly, but tell him I said hello."

"I will do that sir," Sean said.

Back at Sean's apartment, he and Baxter relaxed with a cold beer. "Will is quite a character," Baxter said.

"Yeah. I hope Eden can distill it to thirty minutes without losing anything. Send Eden the interview as soon as possible. Never mind. I'll see if she can come over after work." Sean leaned back in his chair. "I'd love to meet Will's 'club'. I bet they're a hoot."

"No doubt," Baxter said, "but I'm surprised. I didn't think any group could keep their mouths shut these days."

Eden arrived at 4:30 carrying bags of Chinese food. "I thought you might enjoy this," she said as she set the food out.

"Wonderful," Baxter said. "Thanks."

"Somebody must have had a craving," Sean said, smiling at Eden.

"Maybe a little."

They discussed business between bites.

"How many minutes do we have of those gals outside the Chinese restaurant," Sean asked.

"Not too many, but probably 10 at least."

"So we can make a 30 minute episode. Eden, be working on the narrative and order of guests. If you don't mind. Don't give Baxter any words he can't pronounce. Just kidding, Baxter." Sean paused for a moment then said, "On second thought, I'd like the order to be: preacher, nurse, Mickey Mouse voters. Thoughts?"

"I agree," said Eden. "From the sublime to the ridiculous. Perfect."

CHAPTER 37

THE FIRST SHOW

The three worked hard the following week to put together a half hour TV program that looked and sounded professional. Eden's experience was invaluable, and Baxter's baritone was perfect for the narration. Sean pretty much stayed out of it, except for a few suggestions promptly nixed by Eden. Sean took notes and started outlining his first campaign ad. The he sent the file to Jim James at the Farm channel for his opinion and suggestions.

Two days later Jim called Sean with his reaction. "Hey Sean, Jim here. That's pretty darn good for a first try, and by amateurs. I've made a couple of edits—saved the original—and will send the edited version over. I also did a Farm Channel new feature introduction I think you'll like. I'm ready to run it when you give it the go ahead. What time slot did you have in mind? By the way, I loved the Mickey Mouse gals."

"Thanks Jim, I really appreciate it. Can we get a prime-time slot? Say 8 p.m. next Friday? I'd like it to get noticed as much as possible. Also, what credits are you running with it?"

"I put you as the producer/director, Eden as the editor/

designer, and Baxter as the narrator. And prime time slots are always available. We'll just have to bump some soybean reports."

"I didn't do anything Jim. Eden did it all. Change me to creative consultant. Everything else goes to Eden and Baxter."

"I'll do that. Watch for the file tomorrow."

Sean, Eden, Baxter, and Rosetta got together at Sean's the following evening to review the edited video. They all thought the edited version was great and told Jim to go with it. Rosetta was impressed.

"That is really good, you guys. Nice job. When's it going to air?"

"This coming Friday at 8 p.m.," Baxter said. "We're getting together at Sean's place for a watch party. You must come over if you're not working."

"Well, hell yes I'll be there."

At seven the following Friday evening the four got together at Sean's apartment and had pizza and drinks of their choice. By the time eight o'clock rolled around they were all a little buzzed for the show, except for Eden. They all cheered after Jim's introduction, then sat rapt for the rest of the show. It was high fives all around and another round of drinks at the end. Ten minutes later Sean received a message on his OED. It was from Sam Hawley. Sean read it aloud.

"Mr. Duncan, just a note to tell you how much my wife and I enjoyed your program. Well done. We are looking forward to many more."

"Well that was unexpected," Sean said.

"Pretty good review for our first try," Baxter said.

Sean asked the TV to replay the show. "He won't be so enamored with our first campaign ad I'm thinking."

CHAPTER 38

TRAGEDY

The next month was uneventful, save for another half hour TV show which featured Will's interview. Will presented well and the editing was good. Reviews were positive, and from what Jim James told Sean, people were asking for more.

The team did more interviews, including a session recorded at an old Iowa farm estate auction, an interview of an Obie couple chowing down at a Freeburger, and another one of Eden extolling the wonders of the Garcia Presidential Library. That interview included some words from Pedro Garcia. After that show was aired the visits to the library from Iowa Farm residents doubled for several weeks.

Then, Sean and Baxter took the opportunity to interview several visitors who lived at Central Iowa Farm, but who never even knew the library existed. All the interviews were carefully reviewed by Sean and Eden for any comments that could be construed as criticism of the Farm system. The plan was to use them in the upcoming campaign ads.

Eden was into her fourth month when she began to question her lack of morning sickness. She didn't mention it to Sean, but when her cramps and occasional bleeding became worse, she made an appointment with a doctor and asked Sean to meet her there.

"What's going on Eden?" Sean asked. "Is the baby okay?" He had just arrived and found her in the waiting room.

"I don't know. I'm scared to death that something isn't right. I've had no morning sickness and my cramping and spotting have gotten worse."

"Why didn't you tell me?"

"I didn't want to worry you. We'll find out together in a little while." Sean held her hands in his.

An Obie nurse held open the door that led to a long hallway. "Ms. Sprayberry." When she saw Sean get up to follow she said, "Are you the husband?"

"I'm the father," Sean snapped.

"It's okay. I want him with me," Eden said.

They were admitted to an examination room where Eden disrobed, rerobed, and assumed the position. The doctor finally came in. "Hello Eden. I'm doctor Franconi. Please call me Claudia. I've read your questionnaire. You're late seeing an OB/GYN. Why is that?"

"I've had no issues until recently. I've felt pretty good for the most part."

"I'm going to do an ultrasound. It will show how the fetus is progressing and hopefully reveal any issues. Doesn't hurt, but then, you know that. Just a little cold on the tummy."

Eden and Sean stared at the weird images on the ultradef monitor and could barely identify their developing child. The doctor froze the image with a side view of what was in Eden's womb.

"I'm sorry Eden. Your baby is severely deformed. Your body is attempting to rid itself of it. There is nothing that can be done except wait for a miscarriage or extract it. Better here in this environment than elsewhere. You should be able to conceive again."

Eden began crying. "I'm sorry Sean. I'm so sorry."

Sean held his head in his hands, then got up and hugged Eden. "It isn't your fault. We can try again if we choose. Don't beat yourself up."

"What happens to the baby?" Sean asked.

"You have a few options," Claudia replied. "What are your wishes?"

"What are our options?" Eden asked.

"Energy stream, burial, donate to science, or cremation."

Eden lost it. "I want it in a jar of formaldehyde so I can put it on my fucking fireplace mantel!" she screamed. She lay back and hugged her face, body wracked with sobs. After a few minutes, Eden regained a little of her composure.

"I've seen the goddamn funeral services here. I want none of it. No energy stream bullshit. No burial that can't be verified. I want my child's brief existence to matter." Eden was up on her elbows glaring at the doctor.

Dr. Claudia Franconi looked at Eden. A look of sadness crept across her face. "I understand. I think your child can best serve society by allowing an analysis of what went wrong. Was it genetics? Environmental? Or something we have yet to identify. Baby Sprayberry could make a difference."

"Sounds like Farm bullshit," Sean said.

Dr. Franconi turned to Sean. "Some of us still care about the people in our society. We work here, but we don't necessarily toe the company line."

The doctor walked to the door. "I could do the procedure here, but you're too far along. I'll send for a nurse to get you to an operating room."

After the procedure and a couple hours rest Sean and Eden returned to Sean's apartment in silence. Eden was too upset to speak and went into the bedroom.

Sean couldn't think of anything to say that sounded empathetic or appropriate. He was grieving too, but kept it buried. A lot of Sean's feelings were tied up in his father's inevitable grief and disappointment when he was told of the loss of his grandbaby. He suspected that his father wouldn't be around to see another if Eden conceived again.

Sean opened the bedroom door. Eden was under the blankets; her eyes were closed. "Are you sleeping?" he whispered.

"No."

"Eden, this is not your fault. You have been doing everything right. No alcohol or other drugs, not even caffeine, daily exercise. You couldn't have been a better pre-mom. Probably something's wrong with me. Hopefully the lab results will determine a probable cause. Please, please, don't beat yourself up."

Eden began to cry again. "It's not that. I know I tried, and I want to try again. I just can't see how I can face your dad. He was so happy. "

"Eden, if anyone understands the cruelty of life, it's my father. You know he killed his own wife so she could rest in peace. He was sent to prison for what eventually came to be ruled a legal and merciful act. My dad will be upset, and want to comfort you. But he will also know it was just shitty luck."

"I need a drink."

"Wine?"

"A cab please."

Sean opened a bottle of cabernet and poured two

generous servings. "You deserve it," Sean said, handing her a glass. "We'll go up and see him tomorrow."

What started with two glasses ended with two empty bottles.

CHAPTER 39

TOMORROW

The morning was gray and depressing — the permacloud layer thickened every spring — which fit the moods of Sean and Eden as they struggled to wake up from their drunken sleep. Sean got up first and showered. Eden slept another hour. When the Ibuprofen and cold water kicked in, Sean called his dad and said he and Eden would like to stop by. After Eden showered and dressed, they took a robocab to the Presidential Library.

The senator led the two to the sofa, where they sat close together and held hands.

"Coffee?"

"Please."

"I suspect this is bad news," Senator Duncan said, handing them both a cup of coffee. "Both of you look like shit. Pardon my French."

Sean looked at Eden and she shook her head. Sean cleared his throat. "It is dad. Our baby was malformed in utero. The baby had to be aborted."

Senator Duncan's eyes teared up. "I am so sorry. I know it is very hard on you two. I wish I had the words to ease your pain, but I know there is no consolation. Life's a bitch, then you die." The Senator bowed his head. "I'm sorry, that's an old saw I heard when I was growing up. It seems to be true too often. I wasn't making light of what happened. I just don't have any words. I love you, Eden. I so wanted a grandchild. Please don't give up."

"Thank you sir," Eden said, then began to cry yet again.

"Will you have a funeral?"

"No," Sean replied. "Eden had a bad experience with her parent's farm funeral last fall. We donated the fetus for research, hoping they can tell us why this happened. I don't have much hope, but it's better than the alternatives."

"Good for you. Are there any issues going forward?"

"The doctor said there shouldn't be any problem conceiving again. We still want to have a child," Sean said. "Not sure when that will happen, obviously."

The senator smiled. "I should not be of any consequence or consideration in your plans. That should go without saying, but I said it. I'm happy knowing you two are determined to move forward."

"Thanks dad. We appreciate it." Sean reached over and held Eden's hand.

"Thank you, sir," Eden said, then blew her nose.

"Please call me dad."

Eden looked up and smiled. "Okay…. dad."

"Thanks dad. It means a lot to us." Sean squeezed his eyes with his fingers, finally lifting his head. "We do have some good news. It seems our Farm Channel shows have done well, and people are asking for more. I asked you before, but I'll ask you again, what would it take for you to tell your story to the nation? Why not tell the truth after all these years? We'd run it just before the election. I think a lot of people would be interested to hear your story as told by you."

"In today's society? I doubt if anyone is interested. A few nerdy historians perhaps. I'm old news son. American history, tradition, and mythology have all seemed to go by the wayside. I'd like to think some people would be keen to hear my story, but I don't have the ego to give it a second thought."

"I think you're wrong, so please consider it. I have to ask: do you think I'd make a good president?"

The senator looked at this son for a long moment. "Honestly? I don't know. Given what I remember of your growing up, and now what I've come to know, I believe you would. I like how you feel about these abominable farms. I like how you treat Eden. Which, I'd add, is an indication of your unselfishness and empathetic nature. But it's a different game out there. I'm not sure you are electable and I'm not sure you could govern effectively, but not for want of trying. Please don't be offended. I've spent years watching the current society emerge. It's been amazing, sad, and pretty much unbelievable to me. But it is what it is. And from what I see, it is only getting worse. I admire your wanting to change it. I ran for president to prevent the change. I failed, and you will too. I'm sorry son, but that's the way I feel. I hope I'm wrong."

Sean walked to the window and stared out to the mall. He didn't see a thing. "Thanks for your honesty. I really do appreciate it and it doesn't offend me at all. I know what I'm up against. I know the Farms are still a minority as far as the population is concerned, but it's growing, and I want it to stop. The Farm vote has been determining the election results for several cycles. The general populace no longer seems to care. I'll have my shot and, win or lose, I'll know I tried. One way or another people will know our names, and in the future will realize we were right."

The room got quiet for a long minute.

"Would you like some more coffee, Eden," the senator asked.

"No thank you sir... er, dad, I'm feeling a little tired. Sorry to cut our visit short, but I need to go home and lie down."

"By all means. Take good care of her Sean."

"I certainly will, dad."

They hugged goodbye and walked out to the mall. Sean called a cab and they rode back to Sean's apartment.

"Your father was a little hard on you," Eden said. "I thought he'd be a little more encouraging."

"He was honest. I appreciate that. He's right. But I'm not going to quit. If nothing else, it should be an interesting experience."

"Please drop me off at my place. I'd like to be alone for a while."

Sean told the robocab the new address. "Please call if you need anything. I love you, Eden."

"I love you too."

The April day remained gray, chilly, and damp. Sean decided to hole up and spend the day reading and writing. He retrieved his father's essays and read them all. He was impressed with the clarity and honesty of the writing and agreed with the ideas put forth. He took notes and marked several pages with sticky notes. He had to ask his father if he could use any of the material. Most of the essays dealt with the damage the Farms would do, and are doing, to America.

The degradation of humans to vectors of fat did not sit well with Senator Duncan.

I STILL DON'T LIKE IT
by
Senator Darius Duncan

As I sit here in my apartment 20 years after my last presidential campaign, I marvel at the changes I've witnessed over the decades. I live in a country I no longer recognize. The climate, the government, war, transportation, and, yes, the American Farm system, are all so foreign to this old senator. I've watched it all evolve and I wake up a little sadder every day. I'm approaching the end of my stay on this wonderful but abused planet. I won't be waking up sad much longer. Until then I can't help but worry for the children who must grow up and make their way in our distorted society.

I ran for president the first time in 2048 hoping to defeat a man whose ideas were repugnant to me. The problems facing our country then were monumental, but I didn't think President Garcia's solutions were the answer. Truth be told—I struggled to argue that taxing people for being overweight and giving people the opportunity to get fat in exchange for a 'free' living would be the ruination of our democracy. I was soundly defeated. The Farm System became a reality and four years later I ran again hoping that I could point out the farm experiment had failed. It hadn't, and 99% of the farm vote went to re-elect President Garcia. His farms were working. The country had a new source of energy, and I was convicted of murder for loving my wife enough to end her suffering.

Old age, wisdom—the passage of time—soothes the sting of defeat. I ended up being freed from prison and have been taken good care of due to President

Garcia's kindness. We became friends and I grew to admire his vision and determination. We had many good talks before his passing. But I could not, and cannot, get on board with the Farm System. I'm in the minority based on their success and continued growth. People outside the farms are of two types: they either don't care or they don't know. The system has spawned a new type of police—the "Obesity Police"—and a new kind of tax dodger—Obies who don't pay their fat tax. And, of course, a new bureaucracy.

The downside is that the life expectancy for farm residents is 15 years less than those Americans who continue to live 'normal' American lives. Farm residents don't seem to care. And their representatives in government don't do what's best for their constituents, which would be shutting down the farms, but do what's best for themselves and their careers. But it has always been that way, hasn't it?

If I were a younger man, I would continue to fight hard for the changes I believe this country needs in order to regain its standing as an example to the world.

Sean thought that this short essay, with a little tweaking, might make a good campaign ad or at least part of a longer campaign media event. He'd run it by Eden, Baxter, and Rosetta to get their input. But not for a few days. Eden needed her rest and her time to grieve.

CHAPTER 40

THE CAMPAIGN BEGINS

The following morning as Sean was having his second cup of coffee, Eden called.

"Good morning, Sean."

"Good morning, Eden. You're sounding better this morning."

"I'm feeling pretty good. I called the library and said I wouldn't be in for a couple of days. Said I had a bad cold. What are you up to today?"

"I have some ideas for a campaign ad that I'd like to run by the campaign committee. Do feel like company this afternoon?"

"Sure, as long as I don't have to cook."

"Not a problem. If Baxter and Rosetta can make it, I'll have Baxter bring some pizzas or something. How does 5 o'clock sound?"

"That'll work. I'll have enough time to clean myself and this place up a bit. See you later."

Sean called Baxter. "Baxter, can you come by Eden's place at five? I'd like to have a committee meeting… good. See you then. Oh, and bring your two favorite things: food and Rosetta."

Sean arrived at Eden's fifteen minutes early. He gave her a gentle hug. "You're going to have to tell Baxter and Rosetta."

"I know."

Baxter showed up promptly at five with two pizzas and Rosetta. Rosetta carried in a tote with two bottles of wine in it.

"I knew you're not drinking so I thought I'd bring my own."

"I can have a glass. We, um… we lost the baby."

"Oh honey. No. What happened?" Rosetta gave her a teary hug.

"I'm so sorry you guys," Baxter said.

Eden told them the whole story without breaking down. "I think the hardest part was telling Sean's dad. We went to see him yesterday. He was quite sad, of course, but comforting. He hopes we try again." Eden got out some plates, forks, and glasses. "I didn't mean to bring everyone down. Let's eat and get down to business."

Eden, Baxter, and Rosetta liked the essay and voted to have the senator read it in front of a camera for the first campaign ad, followed by Sean smiling, saying "That's my dad. And I agree with what he said. Vote for your best interests. Vote Sean Duncan for president."

"I can borrow a teleprompter from Jim James as well as a small video cam," Sean said. "Since my dad won't leave his apartment, we'll have to shoot it there."

"Are you going to ask him first?" Eden said.

"I'll tell him we want to discuss campaign issues and we'd like to drop by. We'll just happen to have the video making gear with us."

Sean messaged Jim James about the video gear. He got a quick reply. "Jim says the gear won't be available for a couple of weeks. He'll let me know when I can pick it up. I guess we'll have time to convince him to do the spot. If he says yes, we can do some run throughs using an OED cam."

When the team approached the senator about doing the spot, he resisted at first. But after some discussion, the politician in him kicked in and he agreed. "I wonder if anyone will know who I am?" he pondered aloud.

It was Father's Day when the Sean Duncan presidential team toted the video gear up to the senator's apartment to get his video recorded. Senator Duncan insisted that no one bring him any gifts. "I am in need of nothing. Seeing you folks on Father's Day is the best gift." Eden printed out a mushy card from the internet and they all signed it and gave it to him when they arrived. "Thank you. I'm trying hard not to tear up. Don't need bloodshot eyes for the camera."

Baxter set up the camera-mounted teleprompter and tried his best to get the lighting correct in the room. They did one rehearsal and viewed the results on the senator's ultradef TV. "Makeup!" Rosetta shouted. "I need to add some color to the senator's face. Luckily, I brought a makeup kit that I put together just for this occasion. I used to work in a salon."

"Boy does this bring back memories," Senator Duncan said. "It's the one thing I hated about the debates."

"I'll be gentle."

When she finished, she pointed at Sean and said "You're next."

They did two more runs with the senator, then it was Sean's turn. It went well; they got his in three takes also. Eden would do the initial editing then the plan was for Sean and Eden to take the recording to Jim James and let him in on what they were doing. Sean thought Jim would be excited in his own weird way.

"Hi Sean, Eden. What brings you here today?" Jim James greeted his visitors.

"I have a couple of videos I need spliced and edited." Sean looked puzzled. "Is 'splice' even a word in video anymore?"

"The word has hung in there," Jim said. "Whatcha got?"

"What say we go outside for a walk," Sean asked.

"Sure, let's go," Jim replied.

The three of them walked to the nearest Freeburger and got some iced tea. "I need to let you in on what we're doing. But I need to know you won't tell anyone." Sean looked Jim in the eye. "It's important to us. What we're up to will be revealed very soon."

"You got my attention. I love a good mystery and need a little spice in my life. I wouldn't tell anyone what you're doing until you tell me to. So what's going on?"

"This video is my first campaign ad. I'm running for president."

"Just like your father."

"Just like my father."

"I love it. I'll see what you got and let you know if I need anything else. Your secret is good with me. When are you going to announce?"

"As late as possible. Elections seem to have become a

weird game. I almost think the later the better. It seems people vote for the last person they see run an ad. ADD or something. I hope for a memorable blitz. My father is in one video."

Jim's eyes widened. "Your father is alive?"

"Yes, he is. He's been living in the penthouse of the Garcia Presidential Library for decades. He and Jesus became good friends. Since the president died, he's been living like a recluse. It's a long story how I found him. I'll tell you all about it when we get the chance. Top secret, by the way."

"I'd love to meet him," Jim said. "I was a big fan. He was the recipient of my first presidential vote. I'm pumped to see the video."

"I'll see what I can do, but it shouldn't be a problem. He seems to be enjoying his re-emergence, as slight as it's been, so far."

"I'm busy right now but I'll get to it as soon as I can and let you know when it's done. It might be a month or so."

"That shouldn't be a problem. Thanks."

CHAPTER 41

GOODBYE

It was Sunday, July 9th, four months before the election. The campaign committee gathered in Eden's office to watch the video which Jim had dropped off at Sean's apartment the night before. It was better than they expected. Jim had done a good job with the editing. He also added a patriotic intro and ending—waving flags, saluting soldiers, etc. "I think my father will be pleased," Sean said. "Let's take it up and show him."

Sean flipped open his OED and beeped his father. "That's funny. He didn't pick up. Maybe he's in the john. Let's wait a few, then go surprise him."

The four took the elevator to the suite expecting a quiet Sunday visit. Instead, they stepped into a frenzy of guards, police, and hospital personnel. One museum guard ran over to stop them. Sean shoved past her. He spotted Pedro Garcia talking to someone in a white coat with a stethoscope around his neck.

"What's going on?" Sean asked. "Did something happen to my dad?"

Pedro Garcia patted the doctor on his arm and motioned

for Sean to follow him aside. Sean waved at the others to stay back. "What is it?" Sean implored.

"The senator was found unresponsive in his bed this morning. He apparently passed in his sleep last night. The paras tried to resuscitate him but were unsuccessful. I'm sorry Sean."

"Where is he! I need to see him." Sean pushed his way to his father's apartment door and went in. His dad was still in his bed with the sheet pulled over his face. A second paramedic was putting away her equipment. "Are you his son?"

"Yes." Sean responded tearfully. "I want to see him."

The para pulled the sheet down. The senator looked peaceful... and dead. The color had left his face. Sean bent and kissed his father on his cold forehead while tears rolled their way to his chin. He kneeled down and made the sign of the cross, bowed his head, and said a prayer he remembered from his youth, to a god he no longer believed in.

After several minutes Sean gathered himself and went out to tell Eden, Baxter, and Rosetta. Of course they had already heard and all were crying softly. Eden put her arms around Sean. "Oh Sean... I am so sorry and so sad." Baxter and Rosetta hugged him in turn.

Pedro Garcia approached. "Mr. Duncan, can you come down to my office? I'd like to inform you of your father's wishes."

"Yes, but I want my friends to join me."

"Your call sir."

The five sat around the conference table in Garcia's office. He'd sent for iced tea. "I am sorry for your loss Mr. Duncan. I grew to like your father after getting to know him and having some intelligent conversations over a scotch and cigar. He almost had me convinced that the Farms were the worst things that ever happened to America. Almost. Your father made it clear he didn't want the news of his death reported. He also just revised his will to leave what little he had to you. Mostly personal writings. My uncle gave him a spot in his mausoleum. He will be interred there, with a small plaque that simply says "DUNCAN". These were your father's wishes."

"We all want to be there at the interment. I insist on watching as the casket is closed and then put into the vault."

"You've been too long at Central Iowa Farm. We don't do funerals the way they do. Actually, this will be only the second we've done here if you don't count moving Garcia's wife's body after this library was built and dedicated."

Sean looked at the clock on the wall. "Can I get a whiskey?"

Pedro got up and went to the cabinet. "Anyone else?"

"Yes," they said in unison.

"We have a decision to make," Sean said. "Do we still use the video? I think my father would have wanted us to."

They were back in Eden's office sipping whiskey from her stash. "How do we do that without everyone thinking it's a deep fake? It's not like the Library will announce the senator's death and how it all evolved."

"What do you think Baxter? Where's the technology for exposing deep fakes?"

"Not bad. There is a law against deep fakes that seek to harm someone or the USA, but people ignore it anyway. DF scanners usually detect them." Baxter got up and poured himself another sip of bourbon. "I say we run with it after we do a documentary about your father. It should include Will and his buddies telling what they know. Not only would it lend credence to the senator's video, but it would also expose some of the bullshit going on at the Farms."

"I like that Baxter," Rosetta said.

"So do I," Eden said.

Sean poured himself a double and walked to the window. "Yup... yup. I'm all for it. I want my father's story to be told. I want people to know he was right about the Farms. Let's get the documentary started immediately."

The burial ceremony for Senator Darius Oliver Duncan was held in a white tent erected on the President Garcia Mall next to the President Garcia monument. Public access to the mall was shut down early that morning. Unbeknownst to Pedro Garcia, Sean had notified Will and asked him to come and bring his close friends to the interment. He told them to come on foot or park a mile away. They would need to sneak in. They had all arrived the night before and camped out in the mall, out of sight of the SPEYES. Baxter would record the event for use in the documentary. He wore glasses that held a hi-res cam since recordings were strictly prohibited. He intended to interview Will and some of his cronies after the burial. The only other attendees were Pedro Garcia, the Obie guard from the penthouse greeting desk, a coroner, and the senator's personal assistant. A cleric of unknown denomination was to say a prayer. No government officials were present. Sean gritted his teeth.

The casket sat on a catafalque in the middle of the tent. As the ceremony was about to begin Sean stepped forward. "Open the casket please."

"Is that really necessary?" Garcia asked.

"Yes it is. Open it."

The coroner opened the casket and Sean nodded.

The coroner closed the lid, and the cleric began a short prayer and blessing. As he did, Will and his group slowly slipped into the tent. They doffed their caps and held their hands over their hearts. Garcia made a motion toward them, but thought better of it. All was silent as the senator was laid to rest.

"Who are these people?" Pedro was in Sean's face.

"Friends of mine and of my father's. They're here on my invite. It's none of your business, Pedro."

"Yes, it is my business, I run this place. They're all trespassing. I'm having them arrested."

"Go ahead and see what happens. There'll be consequences. I'm tired of the bullshit surrounding my father's last years. I will be telling the truth."

"His NDA extends to his family."

"Prove it."

Sean and his team walked Will's group back to their vehicles. Sean and Baxter asked questions of every one of them. Baxter videoed every word. There was a half dozen men and most had little to say, save for expressing their love of the senator. The senator, besides being an opponent of the Farms, was also a strong supporter of civil rights. Despite the two hundred plus years since the civil war, discrimination still lingered in the hearts of many Americans. These men knew a believer when they saw one.

"I got enough, Sean," Baxter said.

CHAPTER 42

TWO MONTHS TO GO

For weeks following the senator's death the group met most days to strategize and assign tasks. The first order of business was to gather any information about Senator Duncan arriving at Iowa Farm and his subsequent life there.

With only nine weeks to the election things got hectic in a hurry. The plan was to have a one hour special about Senator Duncan air two weeks before voting day, then start blasting out the Senator's campaign ad as often as possible. It would go out on the Farm Channel first, with the hopes that the nationwide news programs would pick it up. They would.

"Baxter, I want you to look up that video you found when we first went to the library. The one where you spot my father arriving at Iowa Farm. We'll use it as the documentary intro."

"Shouldn't be a problem," Baxter replied.

"Eden, do a quick review of the interviews with Will's friends after the burial. Sort of a pre-edit for Jim."

Eden stiffened in her chair and her eyes narrowed. "Uh no, no I won't. I resent that, Sean. I'm capable of putting

216

together a complete and coherent edit of that time slot, and every other time slot. I don't appreciate you selling me short. I signed up to be a big part of this campaign and that's what I expect to be. In addition, I really grew to love your father and I want to do all I can to bring his story to the American people. I can do anything Jim James can do, and probably better. What I can't do is get it on TV."

Baxter and Rosetta flashed raised eyebrows. Sean looked surprised. Eden didn't look away from Sean.

"I was… uh, just trying to save you some work. Put you on something more important."

"You are so full of shit. You're a bad liar. Strap 'em on, or whatever the term is, and make a decision. I'm doing this for your father, not for you."

"You go girl," Rosetta said.

"I, uh, think I'm going to second that," Baxter said.

Sean stood up and lowered his head. "I stand duly chastised. Eden, please take over all the editing and the storyboard. When we all agree that it's ready for prime time, I'll ask Jim for his opinion and suggestions. We need it in two weeks max. Eden, do you have vacation time coming? Or, can you handle this along with your duties here?"

"My duties here take up about a half hour a day. I'll get it done."

"What can I do?" Rosetta asked.

"I would like you to get a copy of my father's death certificate. I was never told the cause of death. I suppose we were all to assume it was old age, natural causes. But I'm curious as to what went on the death cert. If you can't access it from your place of work, maybe Baxter can hack in for you."

"Awright! Cool. I love this shit. I'm on it first thing tomorrow. Are you thinking there might be something nefarious?"

"I doubt it, but I want to cover all the possibilities. I appreciate your help."

"Was there an autopsy?" Rosetta asked.

"There wasn't supposed to be. Try finding that out too."

"Your father couldn't possibly have had any enemies," Eden said.

"You're right, but there could be other factors in play."

"Like what?"

"Budget cuts."

"Seriously?"

"Weirder shit has happened in this country," Rosetta offered. "Garcia General had to lay off a lot of people in the past two years. Despite the rosy Farm reports, the real world is still hurting. I hate to say it, but having the senator gone would save the library a ton of money every year. Old folks aren't respected like they used to be. Whoever runs this place above Pedro might look at it as a mercy killing. Maybe even Pedro. Though he seems like a pretty straight shooter to me."

"Eden, you were hired because of why?" Sean asked.

"I was told the library needed a boost in attendance to cover rising costs and that some fresh adverts and promos would help. Certainly legit, but the financial condition of the library was never mentioned. I'll see what I can dig up. Baxter, I may need your help."

"It's great to be needed," Baxter smiled.

They took a few days off then met again for their Sunday session. Cooler weather and autumn colors marked the start of the harvest. The massive harvesting machines began their weeks-long roar. Diesel exhaust hung low in the air, creating what became to be known as

"Smogtober." Some campaign ads popped up from time to time, but not for the presidential race.

"Greetings all," Sean said. "Baxter, you first. How'd you do?"

"I got the intro vid to Eden as well as some clips of the debates with Garcia. There are several that I thought would highlight your father's intelligence and debating skills. I still can't believe he lost—twice."

"Great. Thanks Baxter. Eden?"

I got a storyboard put together as well as a preliminary voiceover for Baxter to begin practicing. You'll find the EstoryBoard on the electro-easel in the corner. I didn't want to use EstoryBoard for the same reason I still like to read and smell real, dead tree books. But no one makes large flip-chart paper anymore. ``

"Great. We'll review that in a minute. Rosetta?"

"I could not find, even with Baxter's help, any record of your father's death. No certificate, no autopsy. Nothing. It's like he didn't exist. There's not even a record of an ambo run that morning."

"Thanks, Rosetta. Baxter, would you try to hack into Pedro's emails? Or the National Archives and Records Administration? Give it your best shot. I want to know if anything of interest was exchanged prior to my father's death. Thanks."

"Will do."

"Now please show us the storyboard." Sean smiled at Eden.

Eden placed the electro-easel near the conference table and flipped the first blank screen. Underneath was a sketch of an opening page entitled "SENATOR DARIUS OLIVER DUNCAN—THE TRUTH" with the senator's official senate portrait in the background. The pages continued while Eden explained the video to be used with each, as well as a brief synopsis of what Baxter would be saying. The closing shot was of the senator in his apartment hugging Sean.

"Well, what do you think?" Eden asked.

"Holy shit! Eden, that was great!" Rosetta jumped up and hugged Eden before Sean or Baxter could say anything. She spun around and looked wide-eyed at the two men. "Whatcha all think? Huh?"

Eden laughed. "You are such a fangirl. Thank you."

"She's right. Good job, honey," Sean said. "How about you Baxter?"

"I am honored and looking forward to doing the voice-over for this. Great job, Eden."

"Thanks. I should be ready to send it to Jim in a couple of days. I am open to any and all critiques, ideas, and general comments. Please don't hold back. This is important."

CHAPTER 43

POTUS NEEDS A FAVOR

Four weeks before election day Director Hawley asked Sean to stop by his office to discuss an important assignment. Sean arrived the following morning. Sam's assistant brought a carafe of coffee to the conference room with two 20th anniversary Iowa Farm commemorative coffee mugs, which were included with every order of Sean's official history book. The harvest was winding down and the noise level and air quality weren't too bad.

"Good morning Sean. Good to see you." Hawley looked up and smiled. "I continue to enjoy your Farm Channel segments. I think you should interview me. I'd love to tell everyone how life is getting better every day at Central Iowa."

"You called me in for that? You could have Cackled or IMed me. But to tell you the truth, I won't interview you. You are a regular, permanent fixture on the Farm Channel, forever spewing your farm statistics and cropaganda. No one would watch it."

"Cropaganda? Nice. I like it, but you're probably right. Thanks for your honesty. Anyway, as you well know the presidential election is fast approaching. President Dinh would like you to do two or three campaign ads for him, extolling the great job he has done and how he'll continue making America greater than ever. You don't have much time. Sorry for the short notice, but I have confidence you can get it done."

Sean looked at Hawley with a half-smile. Then he looked around the conference room at all his father's books, collecting dust. Quite a collection he thought. His eyes stopped at the row of Hemingway books. His father was a fan and managed to make him one too. He fought back tears.

Sean pulled out a tissue from the box on Hawley's desk and blew his nose.

"You alright?' Hawley asked.

"I'm fine." Sean gathered himself and said "Not gonna happen."

"What do you mean? You need to get this done," Sam said.

"I'm doing my own campaign spots. I'm running for president."

"What? You can't do that."

"Of course I can. I'm an American citizen, older than 35. So, yes, I can and I am. I'll not be doing any campaign ads for President Dinh."

"You risk losing your free ride here at Iowa. I can have you sent back to Farm Jail."

"For what? I don't owe any Fat tax. I've committed no crimes. I'm giving the Farm Channel a reason to exist. So why would you have me in jail? I'm simply exercising my right as an American citizen."

"Who else knows about this?"

"My campaign committee," Sean said. "Eden, Baxter, and Rosetta."

"Rosetta?"

"Rosetta Stone. A nurse at Garcia General. Nice gal. She and Baxter are an item."

"Do you really think you can win?" Sam asked. "You don't stand a chance." Hawley's tone had just a hint of uncertainty.

"Perhaps not. Probably not. But I'm going to try. I'll get my story, and my father's story, out there for the country to see. People will know the truth."

"Your father's story? That's a little past its use-by-date isn't it?"

"A month or so, yes."

"What does that mean?"

"My father died a month ago."

"Your father's been dead for decades."

"C'mon Sam. You must have known. My father lived in the Garcia Library in the penthouse. He and Jesus became good friends. They sat and drank scotch and smoked cigars every evening. The library took care of him and managed, obviously, to keep it a secret. I showed you that these books in this room belonged to him. Why would they be here if he wasn't? This was his library and was brought here when Iowa Farm opened. His arrival was accidentally captured on video during the opening ceremonies. It will be shown on the one hour special I'm doing on Senator Darius Oliver Duncan. It's must-see TV."

Sam Hawley sat expressionless. His eyes darted from Sean's, to the book shelves, and back. "I never knew."

"How could you not know? You married Garcia's daughter."

"I told you she didn't approve of the Farms, and she never went to the library. She totally disagreed with him about the Farms and the Obesity Police."

"She knew. You might want to ask her tonight." Sean got up. "Ask Dinh if he knew, the next time you see him."

At dinner that night at the Hawley's, Sam was quiet. The fact that Senator Duncan had been living under his nose for decades ate at him. Why wasn't he informed? The Presidential Library sat in the middle of Central Iowa Farm and he was the director. He was going to ask some questions of the National Archives and Records Administration.

"What's up hon?" Juanita asked. "You seem a little pre-occupied. Everything alright?"

"I'm fine. I got some interesting news this morning. I'll tell you about it later. Let's enjoy our dinner."

Juanita Hawley, nee Garcia, was an attractive Latina, a bit plump, an Obie actually, but with a borderline BMI, so her Fat Tax wasn't much. She grew up in the New White House with servants and Secret Service all around. She hated it. Home schooled by a liberal free spirit, she was exposed to ideas that excited her and made for heated dis-cussions around the dinner table.

She received a degree in ecological studies from the University of Nebraska and got a job in the Department of Agriculture. It was there she met Sam Hawley and fell in love. They were married after a brief engagement.

Soon after the wedding Sam was appointed Secretary of the Department of Agriculture. Most thought it a great example of nepotism. He worked hard to prove he had earned the job. Then, as soon as the Central Iowa Farm opened, President Garcia selected him to be its director.

The only friction in Sam and Juanita's marriage was the decision to have children. Juanita refused to bring children into the overheated war zone that was the earth. Sam had wanted kids and his father-in-law wanted grandchildren, but Juanita wouldn't budge.

Sam brushed his teeth and crawled into bed with his wife. She was reading a book. Sam turned to her. "Why haven't we ever gone to your father's library?"

Juanita put her book down and turned toward Sam. "I've told you a hundred times. Every time I think about going, I get upset. I loved my father but hated what he did to this country. The library celebrates these stupid farms. I want to remember him as my loving father, not the father of the Obesity Police."

"You remember I told you about Sean Duncan—Senator Duncan's son? He does the Farm Channel promos."

"Sure. What about him?"

"President Dinh asked me to get him to record some campaign ads for him. So I called Sean into my office this morning. He refused to do any ads for Dinh."

"Why not?"

"He's running for president. His father just died a few weeks ago. Senator Duncan had been living in an apartment in the library on the presidential suite level since it was built. He and your father became good friends. Smoked cigars and drank scotch together. At least according to his son."

"He's running for president? Senator Duncan just died?" Juanita got up on her elbow.

"Yes and yes."

"Did you know the senator was living with my father?"

"I did not. I can't believe it was kept from me all these years. Sean thinks you knew. Did you?"

"My father never told me. Maybe he knew I would have announced it to the world. Are Sean's politics like his father's?"

"I'm sure they are. He doesn't stand a chance if he's anti-Farm. The Farm vote has determined the last five presidential elections. Millions of Obies love their lifestyle."

"I want to meet him. I want to tell him I am going to vote for him."

"I'll arrange it." Sam stared at the ceiling. "I may vote for him too. I'm getting a little tired of all the Farm bullshit."

CHAPTER 44

CRUNCH TIME

When Eden received Jim's markup of the hour-long Senator Duncan special, she saw he'd made a few minor tweaks but told Eden that it was great and if she ever needed a job to let him know. She called a meeting of the committee to meet at Sean's apartment that night to watch it.

"Who wants what to drink? I'm making popcorn. There's a charcuterie board, a veggie tray, chips, tapas, and shrimp. Central Iowa giveth."

"I'll have an IPA," Baxter said.

"White wine for the ladies," Rosetta said.

"Beer for me too." Sean poured and passed out the drinks.

Eden had the remote. She dimmed the lights and started the video. It was a quiet hour as the story unfolded.

Sean coughed and wiped his eyes. "Um… give me a minute to gather my thoughts. I'm a little emotional."

"Yeah. No shit. That was in-fucking-credible. Wow." Rosetta high fived Eden. "Makes me want to vote as many times as I can."

"You get one honey. Any more earns you a public beheading," Baxter said.

"Eden, you did such a good job. Thank you. I know my dad would have liked it. I hope it strikes a chord with the voters. I'm thinking it will, especially with those who remember my father."

"Do we follow up each broadcast with our campaign ad?" Eden asked.

"For sure after the first airing. If we don't get shut down we'll keep it up. Play the documentary every night followed by the ad. It should be interesting. I'll get with Jim to see what's possible."

"We should begin the blitz eleven days before election day. That gives us two weekends to shock the country," Eden said. "We must avoid getting shut down. Baxter, I hope you can handle that."

"Once the real web gets ahold of it the Farms can't do a thing. If the Farms shut it down, then I have some back channels I can fire up and continue the broadcasts."

"Real reporters are going to come flooding in here asking for interviews," Rosetta said. "How do we handle that?"

"I don't believe the Farm will allow them access," Sean said. "President Dinh will see to it."

"That would be a first amendment rights violation I believe," Eden said. "Anybody know a good constitutional attorney?"

"This place got lawyers?" Rosetta asked.

"Yeah, but they're all Farm employees," Eden said.

"I know one on the outside. Not sure if he's constitutional. Worked with my folks. I could see if he's still in business."

"Thanks Rosetta. But let's see what happens," Sean said. "Dinh may not care. I'm sure he figures he's a lock."

Rosetta got up and started to clear away the snacks and empty glasses. "We'll see."

"Yes, we will. I'm going to call Jim James first thing tomorrow," Sean replied.

Sean awoke early and made a pot of coffee. He was on his second cup when he called Jim James.

"Good morning Jim. The documentary was great. Thanks so much."

"Eden did a great job. I barely had to touch it. You tell her that."

"I will. She'll appreciate it. We'd like it to run at 9 p.m. Eastern on October 28th. Can you make that happen? And as soon as it's over, run the campaign ad."

"It'll go to the real world as well."

"I figured it would. Thanks so much. How often can it run? I'd like it to go out daily in some time slot."

"I'll try. I might get shut down, but once the rest of the country sees this, especially the older voters, the national news will run it every chance they get, along with their interviews of anyone they can grab off the street. Expect a plague of reporters descending on Central Iowa Farm. Does Hawley know?"

"Yes. I told him when he called me in and said President Dinh wanted me to do some campaign spots for him. I told him I wouldn't, and I told him why."

"Good for you. You'll probably be hearing from Dinh."

"I hope so."

Hanh Dinh was a 5th generation descendant of Vietnamese refugees. Like Jesus Garcia he had worked his way up through California politics and ran for president when Garcia passed on running for a third term. President

Garcia led the movement to repeal the 22nd amendment. Due to the popularity of the Farms and the number of them in the high population states, it only took 18 months to pass the repeal. Hanh Dinh was running for his fourth term. Like Social Security before it, the Farm System had become the third rail of politics and Dinh swore to never allow anyone to shut them down. He never spoke of his personal feelings about the Farms. He was a lean-as-a-rail Rexic whose family owned a successful chain of gyms throughout the country—the Lean Too Corporation. He was also a cutthroat politician who knew how to get his way.

CHAPTER 45

IT STARTS

The next meeting, another TV watching party, took place at Rosetta's apartment. Baxter had been there all day and the two of them ate dinner at five. Sean and Eden arrived at 7. The documentary was due to air in an hour. Rosetta put together snack trays. Baxter swiped snacks when Rosetta's back was turned. Sean paced while Eden helped Rosetta in the small kitchen.

"Here. Drink this." Eden handed Sean a scotch on the rocks, a double.

"Thanks Eden. I have never been this nervous in my life." Sean took a large sip of the whiskey. "I know I've said it before, but I'll say it again, I can't thank you three enough for the hard work you've put in and for your faith in me and for our cause. Win or lose, we will know that we gave it our best shot."

"Sean honey, I think you'll win. I have faith. You should too. Think positive," Rosetta said.

"Thanks Rosetta. I'm trying, but we have literally tons of opposition."

"Megatons," Eden added.

"This country has a history of classes of people voting against their own self interests," Sean said.

"This is different, Sean." It was Eden. "The millions of Obies living on the Farms obviously love it. That is their self-interest. But we think their self-interest should be a healthy, long life. They mostly disagree or are too weak to break the high calorie bonds that hold them."

"Well put Eden," Baxter said. "I've been in the second group—too weak. Rosetta and I plan on getting out of here after the election. We don't want to be married at Central Iowa Farm. Loving Rosetta has given me strength."

Sean and Eden smiled and looked at Rosetta and Baxter. Rosetta had a half smile and stared into her drink. Baxter stood wide-eyed. "Well congratulations you two," Eden said. "Where's the champagne?"

"It's in the freezer chillin'," Rosetta said. She got up and poured everyone a champagne toast.

"Here's to two of the nicest people I've ever had the pleasure of working with. Congrats to both of you and may your future be joyous, fruitful, and serene." Sean raised his glass.

At 8 p.m. the documentary started. The Sean Duncan for President campaign committee members each took a deep breath. Of course, they had seen it multiple times, but knowing the nation would be seeing it was hard to grasp. Before it was half over Sean's OED began to pulsate. He had messages from Sam Hawley, Juanita Hawley, Jim James, Pedro Garcia, all the major media networks, and all the minor ones. He opened one from the BBC.

They wanted an interview.

Everyone wanted an interview.

After the documentary ran, the Sean Duncan for

President ad ran. Sean's OED was under a new assault. This one included a message from Hanh Dinh.

"I just got a message from the POTUS," Sean said.

"What'd he say?" Rosetta asked.

"I'm afraid to open it."

"Awe, go on you chickenshit. It's probably a congrats-hope-you-win message."

"Not likely," Sean said. He tapped his OED and read the message.

"Well, he did congratulate me on my effort, but said my father's ideas have not resonated for decades and that he will prevail, as he puts it, in the election."

"He's not sending the Obesity Police, is he?" Baxter asked.

"Didn't say. If he thinks I stand a chance, which I don't think he does, he'll send out far more nasty people. Despite the resurgent populist sentiment in the country, the wheels of government continue in the ruts of the past. Most people vote just to get a discount at their favorite etailer."

"Pretty cynical, Sean," Eden said.

"I wish it were. I'm afraid it isn't."

"Read another one!" Rosetta said. "What did Hawley have to say?"

Sean tapped his OED and read the director's message. "Interesting. Hawley said good job, very well done and professional. Asked me to come in on Monday to discuss some things."

"Uh oh," Baxter said.

"Then he said, 'things I think you'll appreciate'."

Sean kept a low profile as the requests for interviews continued unabated. The documentary and campaign ad ran several times on Sunday before the Farm Channel shut it down. Sean and Eden hunkered down in his apartment and watched the nation's reaction to the news about Senator Duncan and Sean's candidacy. Sean was amazed at the outpouring of love for his father. Of course, most of the interviews were not with people who were in a government farm. People outside, the older ones, remembered him fondly and said they had voted for him. Others said they voted for Garcia but not because of his weird farm idea. Sean couldn't help but wonder why his father didn't win— especially the second time he ran.

Then the Farms struck back.

The attack ads started that Sunday at 5 p.m. on local news channels and the Farm Channel.

Many of them were a version of 'would the real Sean Duncan please stand up' which pointed out all the Farm promos he had done. They also ran ads solely on the Farm Channel saying that, if elected, Sean Duncan would shut down your way of life. Sean never thought he could win the Farm vote anyway.

On Monday morning Sean walked to the Welcome Center to meet Sam Hawley. He was praying that he wasn't getting fired.

CHAPTER 46

TWO WEEKS TO GO

Sean sat in Hawley's office working on his second cup of coffee. The Director finished something on his computer and pushed the keyboard out of his way. "Good show last night. Unfortunately, I had to fire Jim James. Boss's orders."

"Shit. I liked him," Sean said.

"He'll do alright on the outside. Talented guy."

"I'll have to give him a call and apologize for causing him to lose his job. You asked me over to tell me that?"

"Oh no. I had a few things to discuss. Also, my wife Juanita is stopping by in an hour or so. She wants to meet you. She's a fan. But first I wanted you to know how upset I was after the information about your father came out. I feel that the Garcia Library should have let me know. I know it's officially not part of Central Iowa, but it sits in the middle of it. And my wife is Garcia's daughter. She was just as shocked as I was at the news. Anyway, I've always been neutral about the Farm System. It's given us a good living, certainly, but Juanita hates the whole concept and I'm having second thoughts. I'm considering voting for you myself."

"Well thank you Sam. I always thought you were gung-ho about your Farm. Thinking of retiring?"

"Maybe. But first I'd like to find out why me and my wife were kept in the dark about your father."

"Now that I got your vote, can I have your confidence?" Sean asked. "As in what's said here stays here?"

"Yes. I'm not interested in talking to anyone in Farm Administration now anyway. So what is it?"

"I think my father was murdered."

Sam sat up straight and leaned toward Sean. "Why do you think that?"

"My dad was healthy for his age. He didn't complain about anything except his arthritis. I'm sure he would have told me if he was having any serious problems. Then out of the blue he dies in his sleep. My team and I happened to be going to visit him the morning of and walked in on the scene outside his suite. Rosetta, Baxter's fiancé, is a nurse at Garcia General. I had her and Baxter do some checking. There was no death certificate, no autopsy, no cause of death, no record of an ambulance run—nothing anywhere."

"Interesting," Hawley said. "But that doesn't mean he was murdered. What would be the motive?"

"Money. The Library was having financial problems and my father's room and board couldn't have been cheap."

"I can't believe that. If he was murdered, it'd have to be for some other reason, and I can't think of one." Hawley leaned back.

"How about this? Someone found out about the documentary and my presidential run and didn't want my father available for interviews or campaign ads."

"Who?"

"POTUS?"

"You're kidding, right?"

"The president had to have known my father's where-abouts and his situation. If he was informed of the documentary and my run, he might have decided to do away with an old man he thought may give him re-election problems. It's a wild theory, but I know POTUS is ruthless."

"I didn't tell anyone Sean, except Juanita."

"I believe you. But I have a favor to ask. In your poking around trying to see why you got left out of the Senator's secret, you should talk to Pedro Garcia, the library director. During your conversation ask him the cause of my father's death. Watch his reaction closely. I think he's your wife's second cousin or something, so you have an in."

"I will do that," Sam said. He looked at his OED. "Juanita's here."

Sean stood up to shake her hand. She pushed through that and gave him a hug. "I'm so sorry for your loss. And I thank you for running for president. I'll be voting for you."

"Thank you Ms. Hawley," Sean said, stepping back.

"No, no, please call me Juanita."

"Okay Juanita. Please call me Sean."

"When Sam told me about Senator Duncan and your campaign I was saddened and excited. Perhaps my husband told you about my feelings about the Farms—I hate them. My father and I never agreed. I refused to visit him in his library. It was a bad time for us. He visited Sam and me occasionally. We didn't discuss the Farms and avoided the rift between us. He never mentioned your father." Sean and Juanita sat down.

The room grew dimmer as a late October storm approached, the skies growing dark as the wind kicked up.

"Used to be snow years ago," Sam said. "Now it's just

warm rain. I guess it's good for the orange groves in southern Iowa."

"I assume you're running as a Lib," Juanita said. "Your father was a good one."

"If by Lib you mean anti-Farm, then yes, although the old labels no longer apply. The new voting rules and regulations made the two-party system disappear. Now it seems to be every man for himself. Pretty weird." Sean looked out at the growing storm. "Wait. Did you say orange groves?"

"They started an experiment ten or so years ago. The southern Iowa climate was deemed warm enough to try. The trees are doing well. Grapefruit trees were next and, from what I hear, they're doing okay. Central Iowa is now growing healthy crops of peanuts too."

Sean stood up. "I gotta get going. I want to run over and see Jim before he packs up and disappears. Juanita, it's been a pleasure meeting you. Thank you for your kind words and support. Sam, thank you too. Let me know what you find, if anything."

Sean walked out and summoned a robocab. "Farm Channel offices, please," he said aloud to no one. The cab proceeded to deliver him to his destination.

Jim James was packing up his office when Sean knocked on the door and walked in. "Hello Jim."

Jim looked up and smiled. "Good morning Sean. You must have heard."

"I did. I'm sorry I got you into this. I didn't think they'd fire you."

"Don't blame yourself. I knew there was a risk. I'm just glad it ran." Jim motioned for Sean to sit down and then sat himself. "I am really sorry about your father. Was it a surprise? I mean, had he been ailing? He looked pretty good in the video."

"That's one of the reasons I'm here. He was pretty good. Between you and me, I think he was murdered."

"Really? Why would anyone do that?" Jim asked.

"Did POTUS or one of his people ever get a hold of you and ask about my video? I mean before anyone knew."

Jim blanched. "Why do you think that?"

"Because I think President Dinh thought my father might cause issues for his reelection."

"His office did contact me. They already knew what I, we, were doing. They just told me to cease and desist or there would be consequences. Of course I ignored them. So out I go."

"Why didn't you tell me?"

"They told me to keep my mouth shut. I thought I better not ignore that. I should have. I can't believe they'd kill him for that."

"Dinh is ruthless. I can't prove it yet. Maybe never, but I'll keep digging into it." Sean got up. "I'll leave you to it. When you leaving?"

"Couple of days. I have a couple of interviews lined up in the real world."

"Best of luck, and thanks for all your help."

CHAPTER 47

THE ELECTION

Besides Hanh Dinh and Sean Duncan, there were a half dozen or so candidates that ran ads on the national networks. The pundits and talking heads all agreed that Dinh was a shoo-in, but they were grateful that Sean got in the race to generate some interest. It was the need to churn constant news that kept Sean's campaign video running on the Web, cable, and satellites.

Voting started on the Sunday before Election Day, which fell on November 7th. Returns started coming in on November 5th. Polls closed at midnight on the 7th. The results were announced soon thereafter. The three election days were the busiest shopping days of the year due to the additional discounts offered if a shopper showed his "I voted" credential.

Eden, Baxter, and Rosetta had jobs to go to, while Sean spent the week searching for any information he could glean about the Library building as well as how the human fat got transported and where it ended up in each building that had extraction and collection facilities. He didn't reveal this activity to Eden.

On the evening of the 6th, Baxter and Rosetta went to Sean's apartment to watch the returns. Eden got out some munchies and drinks. By 9 p.m. Dinh led Sean 52% to 48%, with the remaining votes scattered among the other candidates.

"Holy crap," Rosetta said. "That is damn good!"

"It's better than I expected, actually," Sean said. "I'd like to be able to say I beat Mickey Mouse."

"You're a lock for that," Baxter said.

"Why isn't the Farm vote separated out? Anyone know?" Eden asked.

"I believe the Farm vote is not released until all the polls close. Then there's a big data dump to the real world," Baxter said.

"No wonder it's so close," Sean said.

At 11 p.m. the watch party ended. They planned to get back together at noon on Election Day for an all-day bash.

Monday the results were little changed with both Dinh and Sean picking up a percentage point while the no-names all slipped a little. The Farm percentages remained unknown. At day's end 58% of the populace had cast their ballots. At noon on the 7th Dinh had a narrow lead and the all-day bash became a celebration of possibility.

"I hope enough Obies came to their senses and voted Duncan," Rosetta said. "We should get most of the Rexics, I think."

"That's a long shot," Sean said. "A lot of Rexics make a decent living working on the Farms.

All evening Sean closed the gap with every update. The 9 p.m. results showed Sean Duncan leading Hanh Dinh by 2 percentage points.

"Woo Hoo!" Rosetta yelled, jumping to her feet.

Eden got up and hugged Sean, who was pacing the room.

Baxter proposed a toast.

Sean fought back a glimmer of hope.

At 9:10 Sean received a message from Will: *Me and the boys are praying for you. Your father is beaming in heaven.* Sean wiped a tear from his cheek.

At 12:01 the next morning the Farms started reporting their vote totals. By 1:00 a.m. it was clear to the team that Sean had lost. The Farms sent Dinh back to the White House, preferring him to Sean by 80% to 20%.

Mickey Mouse received 928,451 write in votes. The celebrants were silent as the numbers rolled in. Eden, Baxter, and Rosetta each hugged Sean, tears in their eyes. No one got any sleep.

Wednesday morning Eden, Baxter, and Rosetta all called in sick. Sean texted POTUS with his congratulations. He received a thank you. He also agreed to a 5 p.m. news conference arranged by the Farm Channel acting director.

The interview took place in front of Sean's apartment building per his request. There was the interviewer, a cameraman, and a satellite truck.

"How are you feeling today, Mr. Duncan," the newsman asked.

"I'm feeling grateful to the millions of people who voted for me," Sean said.

"Why do you think you did so poorly in the Farms?"

"People like their comfort food. I'm proud of what we did in the real world. To gather so much support in such a short amount of time was phenomenal."

"What's next for you?"

"I'm going to take a break and do some writing. I've a lot I want to say. I will stay engaged with those who supported me. I want to see this country on a better road to the future. I believe one exists."

CHAPTER 48

SMOKING GUN

Sean took it easy for the next few weeks. He exercised every morning; began writing a book about his journey from meeting Eden in Old Detroit to his presidential election run. He received a notice that he would be required to pay rent on his apartment starting the first of the year. He thought it was nice of them to give him another rent-free month.

Three weeks after the election Baxter rapped loudly on Sean's door. It was late afternoon on a cool, damp, late November day.

"C'mon in Baxter," Sean said. "I wasn't expecting you."

"I wasn't expecting to be here," Baxter said. "I've got some news. Where's Eden?"

"At work. Sit down. Can I get you something to drink?"

"I need a whiskey, rye, a double."

"Must be serious."

Sean poured Baxter's drink and one for himself. They sat at the dining table. Baxter opened the backpack he had been wearing and retrieved a manila folder. He sat back in his chair and stared at Sean, catching his breath.

"Jeez, Baxter. Calm down. What gives?"

"I found it, Sean."

"Found what?"

"The smoking gun. Your father was murdered."

Sean's face tightened, grew dark. His hands trembled as he clenched his fists.

"Are you sure?"

"I've been digging since Election Day. Eden gave me access to her office and computer. I went through thousands of files, messages, data – anything I thought might reveal anything related to your father. After a lot of work I managed to hack into Pedro's messages. I did searches with what I thought were good words, things like *senator, duncan, overhead, garcia library, penthouse expenses,* and anything else I could think of. Nothing came up until I realized I could narrow my search to a few weeks. Duh. So I retrieved every message from the prior two weeks before your father's death. And I read all 4,278 of them."

Sean leaned forward.

"What did you find?"

Baxter pushed a printout across the table. Sean's hand was still shaking as he picked it up and read it: *We can no longer afford the old expense.*

"Son of a bitch! Those fuckers." Sean downed his drink and got up and poured himself another and poured more for Baxter. His hands were trembling to where he spilled the rye whiskey all over the table.

"I'm going to get my revenge. They'll be sorry. I'm going to get my revenge."

"This note isn't proof Sean, although you and I know it is. I tried to find the origin, but couldn't. Also, there wasn't a reply as far as I could tell."

"No reply, but certainly a response." Sean sat back down and took a deep breath. "I know you and Rosetta are leaving soon. But I'd like your help one last time. Any chance of that?"

"You know I will. What can I do?"

"I'd like you to get me a copy of the design drawings for the Garcia Library basement – where the diesel generators are. Also, I want to know how the human fat arrives at the collection points in the buildings and then on to the main vats, or however it's stored. Is it pumped? Does it drain? If so, how does that work? Anything you can find. I tried to research all that but came up empty. Yes?"

"Hmm... I get the feeling I may be aiding and abetting."

"You may be, but you've done it before old friend."

"True, but now I need to guarantee my clean exit from this place."

"Just get me the prints. I'll handle it from there."

Baxter sipped his rye and gave Sean a long, quiet look. "You're going to blow something up."

Sean and Baxter exchanged stares. Sean slowly nodded his head. "Maybe."

Baxter got up and went into the kitchen and grabbed a bag of pretzels and a beer.

"You want something while I'm up?"

"I'm good. Thanks," Sean said.

They were quiet for several minutes as they sipped their drinks and gathered their thoughts.

"I want in," Baxter said.

"No you don't. I don't want you risking your neck for me. You have Rosetta to consider. Just get me that information and get your ass out of here."

"No, I want in," Baxter said. "You have made my life interesting. I like it when my life is interesting. Tell me the plan."

Sean motioned to Baxter to go with him on a walk.

CHAPTER 49

GETTING READY

As soon as they got far away from the building, Sean swore Baxter to secrecy. Steam rose as they walked and whispered. Sean admitted that Eden had no hint of how he was plotting his revenge. If Baxter was to be a part of it, he had to let Rosetta know their move from the farms would be delayed a month or so. "Would that work?"

"I can make it work. I'll tell her I need to finish a good paying job I agreed to—a complete technical upgrade to the Garcia Presidential library. She can leave early if she wants. I'll meet her after the job." They were planning to move to Omaha before Christmas, where Rosetta still had some family. They felt confident they could find work and buy a house.

"I thought the library was hurting for money," Sean said. "How can they afford that?"

"They got a chunk of change tacked on to an appropriations bill or something. I don't really know. Anyway, Rosetta is not going to leave here without me. I'm sure of that."

"Thanks Baxter. You found yourself a good woman. Take care of her."

The two friends hugged and departed company.

Sean and Eden lay in bed after some uninspired love-making. Sean was preoccupied with his thoughts of revenge. Eden was aware of his mood and thought some sex might cheer him up.

"Didn't help, did it?" Eden asked.

"It usually does. Sorry I'm such a dud this morning. I know I've not been myself. Thanks for reminding me how much I love making love to you."

The Sunday dawn oozed grayness into the December sky. It was quiet in their building; most people were still asleep or camped in front of their ultradefs, mesmerized by their favorite show. Miles away a tractor started, warming up to begin turning the earth in preparation for next season's planting.

"You've been quiet lately," Eden said. "Still smarting from the election?"

Sean stared at the ceiling. "No. I'm still smarting from my father's unexplained death."

"Still think he was murdered?"

"I do. But I can't prove it."

"Has any evidence turned up?"

"Not yet." Sean lied.

"Assuming you had proof, what would you do?"

"I don't know."

Sean broke the ensuing silence. "What should I make for breakfast? I'm getting hungry."

Eden rolled over and hugged Sean. "Let's leave this fucking farm. I'm sick of tractors in the morning."

"We will, and soon."

Eden kissed him on his chest. "Good. Eggs Benedict."

"Coming right up."

Sean got a quick shower and went in to start breakfast.

Eden took her time, and the breakfast was ready when she was.

"Baxter's coming over to watch football with me. You and Rosetta got plans?"

"We are going downtown for lunch and a little shopping."

"Good for you. Too bad the day is so gloomy."

"Most of them are this time of year."

After the ladies left, Sean and Baxter sat down with beers and snacks. Baxter tuned the TV to a couple of games featuring the Lions vs. the Packers and the Patriots vs. the Buccaneers. He muted the sound. Then he did a quick check of the apartment with his electronic scanner, searching for a possible bug. He found none.

"Can't be too careful," Baxter said as he plopped onto the couch.

Sean sat down and turned to Baxter. "I was considering bombing the library and maybe a collection site. Then I realized I had no idea how to make a bomb and couldn't research it without men with large weapons breaking down my door. Also, I don't want to kill anyone. Well maybe Pedro Garcia, but really, not even him. Just want to make him miserable for a while."

"I'm glad to hear that," Baxter said. "So how do we make him miserable?"

"Burn down the library."

CHAPTER 50

RECONNAISSANCE

Sean and Baxter met at the library on Monday at noon. Eden was in her office, but the two didn't visit her. Instead, they took the elevator to the lowest floor available to them. They were seeking the basement where the big diesels pounded away day and night providing electricity to the library. The library was scheduled to be connected to the Farm grid, but the conversion never occurred due to funding squabbles between the American Farm Administration and the National Archives and Records Administration. They did reach an agreement on the price of biodiesel fuel to run the generators.

The two had borrowed maintenance uniforms from the basement of their apartment building, which they were wearing as they stepped out of the elevator. They had also donned caps to prevent identification by the SPEYES. Via Eden, in an unrelated discussion, Baxter had learned that the SPYE monitor room was seldom staffed due to recent budget cuts. Being flagged and identified seemed a remote possibility. The basement was poorly lit and noisy. They heard the diesel engines thumping somewhere ahead of them. That's where they headed.

The power room was behind a set of double steel doors. A sign on the door read "AUTHORIZED PERSONNEL ONLY." The doors were ajar. The room was large, damp, and dirty. Spider webs hung from the rafters and mouse shit was everywhere.

"Well, I'm certainly not impressed with the security," Baxter said.

"No kidding," Sean said. "But then, how many people want to burn down a library?"

There were two 16-cylinder diesel generators in the room. Only one was running and the sound was deafening. Baxter took photos from every angle. He shot pictures of the fuel feeds, exhaust pipes, and anything else he thought would be useful. The fuel lines entered the room through the wall and ran level to the motor fuel intake. They were black pipe, like natural gas lines in residential homes.

"What do you think?" Baxter asked.

"This should be easy," Sean said. "We just need a drill."

"I didn't bring one."

"I know. We'll bring one next trip. Here's what I'm thinking: We drill a small hole in the fuel feed line, which happens to be near the exhaust manifold. At some point the leaked fuel should ignite, if we get the leak going in the right direction."

"How do we drill a hole in a steel pipe without igniting the fuel?"

"Dribble water on it as we drill very slowly."

"Could work," Baxter said. "We could add some sort of redirection to get it to drip on the exhaust manifolds." Baxter thought about it for a minute. "I still don't think the fire will big enough to destroy the building before it's put out. We'll need a bigger leak."

Baxter walked around the big engine, looking at the fuel lines.

"We'll bring a pipe wrench. I can undo the main fuel line fitting to the non-running engine. A lot of fuel on the floor in a flash. Pun intended."

"We'll need a fuse of some kind," Sean said. "We shouldn't need more than a couple of minutes to get out."

"I'll work on that," Baxter said. "When do you want to do it?"

"We'll decide later. Let's get out of here and review the pics. I'm getting a little antsy."

They were back at Sean's place after having shed the maintenance uniforms and dumped them in Sean's closet for later use. They did a quick review of the pictures on Baxter's OED. Casting them to the ultradef would compromise their security. Baxter had been careful to take his device offline.

"Maybe we should just let it leak until the basement's half full of biodiesel," Sean said.

"That won't work. That's a zillion gallons of fuel. It's a big room. Besides, how do we ignite it? It will never reach the exhaust manifolds before the leak is discovered," Baxter said. "I think the fuse is the best bet for ignition. When do we need it?"

"When are you and Rosetta leaving?"

"When we finish our project at the library. How about you and Eden? You guys are going to want to leave in a hurry. Someone will be wondering if you had anything to do with it."

Sean looked at the calendar on his OED. "Two weeks until Christmas eve. That gives Eden enough time to turn in her resignation and me enough time to tell Hawley I'm leaving for vacation during the Holidays."

"And when you don't return?"

"I'll have to watch my back."

CHAPTER 51

WHERE THERE'S SMOKE

Later, when Eden got home from work, Sean had dinner ready; lasagna, crusty bread, tossed salad, a nice California cabernet.

"What's the occasion?" Eden asked as they sat down to eat.

"We're leaving in two weeks."

"Two weeks? How will we be ready in time? Why the short notice?"

"You said you wanted out of this place. We're getting out. It's not like we have a lot to take with us. Just our clothes basically." Sean picked at his food. "By the way, where's your Honda?"

"The police put in storage when I went to jail."

"Any problem getting it out?"

"Just a storage fee probably. If it's still there. I'll check on it tomorrow. I haven't needed it so I just left it in storage."

"I'm going to see Hawley tomorrow. He should know where it is. I'll ask him to have it delivered here, see what he says. By the way, don't' resign yet. I may want to get in after hours to grab some stuff from my father's apartment."

"I don't think it would matter. The library is open 24/7/365, but there's always a guard at the main entrance."

They finished dinner and cleaned up. Sean debated telling Eden what he and Baxter were planning but decided against it. He didn't think she would handle it well. It will be all over the news on their trip back to Michigan.

That evening Sean beat Eden to bed. After she had brushed her teeth and came out of the bathroom Sean said, "Get naked."

"Really?" Eden said. "Two days in a row?" She slipped out of her nightgown and slid in next to Sean. "You must be feeling better."

"Much better. It's the feeling you get after you've made a big decision."

Sean stopped by the Welcome Center without telling Sam he was coming. He didn't want Sam to put him off. Sean walked up to the entrance he felt the memory of his first time here come flooding back. It seemed like a lifetime ago. He sent a message, letting Sam know he was in the lobby.

Sam came out and greeted Sean. They walked to the conference room.

"Sorry to drop in unannounced. I'll only take a minute of your time."

"How are you getting along Sean? Recovered from the election yet?'

"Pretty much. Just taking it easy. Doing a little writing." Sean looked around one last time at his father's books. "Eden and I are going to take a couple weeks off and visit some of my old friends in Michigan. Leaving on Christmas Eve. Can you have her Honda dropped off at my place? She said the police put it in storage when she went to jail."

"She hasn't picked it up yet?"

"Said she didn't need it, which she didn't. She left it where it's safe."

"I'll do that for you. But listen, just be sure you come back. You're still under contract to the Farms. Although I'm not sure what your role could possibly be. We'll probably be making a clean break."

"Yes we will," Sean said. "Is Baxter working here today?"

"I believe so. Probably in the IT lab."

"Thanks, I just want to see him for a minute."

Sean left Hawley's office and found Baxter at his desk. "Nice day, my friend. Come take a break with me. Let's go out for a walk."

"Sure. The weather's warm enough."

When they reached the edge of the parking lot, Sean said, "Christmas Eve, 4 am. Tell Rosetta to turn in her resignation and pack. Get your bus ticket. We have Eden's Honda. Sorry, you two won't fit. Did you find a fuse?"

"Wow. Okay. I found a piece of sisal rope. I'll saturate it with charcoal lighter. It'll light and burn slow enough. How are we going to get in the building?"

"I thought you could hack into the library's system and unlock the doors and turn off any alarms."

"I can do that."

"Thanks. You better get back to work."

Later, Baxter took a robocab to pick up Rosetta at the hospital when she got off her shift. The car dropped them off at the Chinese restaurant where they first met. It wasn't crowded and they chose a booth in a corner. The décor hadn't changed a bit and the aroma brought back memories of that evening when Baxter found the courage to speak to Rosetta. He held her hand in his and smiled. She smiled back.

"This was a good idea, Baxter," Rosetta said. "Good vibes here."

"Looks the same. Smells the same. I don't hold out much hope for improved food."

"What did you get the first time?" Rosetta asked.

"Unlimited buffet. I think I went up three times."

"You keep it to one tonight, honey. Don't need to be plumping up now."

Later, at Rosetta's place, Baxter told her, "Sean and Eden are leaving early on Christmas Eve. They found her car and are heading for Michigan. I'd like us to leave the same day. What do you think?"

"I am so ready to get out of this shithole and go back to Omaha. I'll let 'em know at work tomorrow and start packing tomorrow night. Have you checked the bus schedule?"

"Not yet. I will."

"Sean, I have a problem." It was Baxter at Sean's door, five minutes after Eden left for work. He'd been waiting for her to leave.

Sean put his finger to his lips, reminding Baxter to speak softly. Sean turned the microwave fan on high. "Come in Baxter. Have some coffee. What's up?"

They sat side by side at the kitchen table. "I can't get a bus out of here on Christmas Eve. Just the day before. I can't risk being here when the shit hits the fan."

Sean thought for a minute, then put his hand on Baxter's shoulder. "Yes, you need to get going if that's all you can get. I will take care of business."

"Are you sure you can get that fitting loosened up? I'm heavier than you and my fat ass hanging off the end of a pipe wrench should bust loose most old fittings."

Sean laughed. "Tell you what. Let's make a dry run this coming Monday at noon. We'll get the joint loosened up and you can give me the fuse. We can leave the pipe wrench there. Speaking of which, where do we get a pipe wrench?"

"I'll get one from the Welcome Center basement. Maybe I'll run into Will. It would be nice to see him," Baxter said. "I'm sorry Sean, I hate to leave you to do this alone."

"It's not your fault Baxter. Or for that matter, your beef. Now, at least, you won't be at the scene of the crime if things go south. Relax, I can handle it."

The day before the dry run Baxter had found a large pipe wrench in Will's area but didn't see Will. He also picked up an apron and some gloves. The dry run went off without a hitch. The pipe fitting broke free easily enough. Baxter had brought a gallon size plastic bag with the fuel-soaked sisal rope. They left that hidden, along with the pipe wrench, apron and gloves, behind a stack of dusty boxes labeled "SAVE".

"You only have one more hurdle," Baxter said.

"What's that?"

"How do you get this done without Eden knowing?"

"I've got that covered. We'll be stopping by the library on our way out of town so I can grab a few items I wanted to save from my father's apartment. I'll tell her to watch the car while I run in. Only be a minute. I told her not to resign or give up her keycode, but it turns out the library is always open for staff. Surprised we didn't know that. Anyway, thanks for asking."

Baxter looked away. His life took a positive twist when he walked into Sean's prison apartment. He felt he was losing his best friend and didn't know how to express his gratitude and mask his sadness. "Will you stay in touch?" he asked.

"I will, although it may be a while. You've been a great friend. I don't want to lose that bond. If I don't get busted, I'll find you. We'll have a reunion. I promise."

"Thanks man." Baxter choked back the tears.

CHAPTER 52

LEAVING CENTRAL IOWA FARM

They had packed the car on Christmas eve and Sean told his OED to wake him at 3:30. He wanted to be on the road before sunrise.

"Why are we leaving so early?" Eden asked. "It's four in the morning."

"I need to stop at the library before we head out. There's a photo in my father's apartment I want to grab. Only take a minute."

"Why didn't you ask me to get it for you?"

"Just remembered it lying awake last night. It's important to me."

"It's probably gone by now."

"I have to check."

They looked around the apartment one last time and closed the door. The Honda Earth was gassed up and packed to the ceiling. They pulled into the library delivery area twenty minutes later. "I'll be right out honey. Sit tight."

Sean tried the closest door. It opened into a large bay. Dim night lights barely illuminated the gray block walls. Sean listened for the diesel. The sound led him to a stairwell. He descended into the basement as his pulse accelerated. Once in, he retrieved the stash from behind the boxes. He pulled on the latex gloves, and put on the apron, grabbed the pipe wrench and wick, and approached the quiet second engine. He pulled the soaked sisal out of the bag and laid it from beneath the fitting to the doorway. He turned the fitting slowly until the fuel began dripping. With his left hand he applied pressure to the pipe so it would point away from him if it let go completely. He loosened it until the leak was substantial, left the wrench gripping the pipe and ran to the door. He threw away the gloves and apron, pulled the lighter out of his pocket, lit the rope, and ran up the stairs. He checked himself for diesel odor but didn't think he got any on him. After a deep breath he walked out and got in the car.

"That was fast. Where's the photo?"

"It was gone," Sean said. "I blew it. Should have got it a month ago."

"I'm sorry, honey."

They made the Iowa Wisconsin border as the sun was rising behind a light layer of the omnipresent clouds. Sean planned his route to keep him off the Interstates. He headed northeast to pick up US 2, the route through Michigan's Upper Peninsula, then across then Straits of Mackinac and south on US 23 toward Detroit.

Eden slept for the first couple of hours. She woke up when Sean stopped at a rest area to pee. When they were rolling again Eden turned on the radio. It was still tuned to a satellite feed of NPR.

"…the fire has engulfed the entire building. Firefighters

are on the scene trying to contain the massive blaze. Once again, the President Garcia Presidential Library caught fire this morning and is probably a total loss. The library is in the middle of Central Iowa Farm but is an independent entity." Eden turned off the radio and stared out the window for a long while. Lake Michigan rippled in the distance casting white sparks off the wave crests. She turned to Sean.

"You didn't...."

Sean gave Eden a quick glance. His face betrayed no emotion as he turned back to the road.

"It's a start."

ACKNOWLEDGMENTS

It took me a long time to finish this novel, and I could not have done it without the help of some wonderful people. When I began this project, I belonged to the Ann Arbor Area Writers' Group. They were honest, kind, and encouraging. Great writers and critics—the lot of them.

My novel sat for years as I struggled to find a direction for it. A few years ago, I attended the Bear River Writers' Conference at Camp Michigania on Walloon Lake in northern Michigan. There, during a session led by Jerry Dennis, and surrounded by a talented group of writers, the direction I needed to go came to me. Many thanks to that inspiring group. In case you don't know, Jerry Dennis is an award-winning author of many books about Michigan and the Great Lakes.

During that same conference I met professional editor Mary Holden. Mary edited this book and made it much better with her skills and knowledge. Thank you Mary.

After my move to Charlevoix, Michigan, I started a writers' group and named it 'Charlevoices'. Some very good writers joined and they helped me improve my work. Thanks to Kenn Grimes, Tom Conlan, Art Curtis, Ebony Parish, Richard Seibert, and Thalia Ferenc.

Kenn Grimes was a beta reader, as was Jennifer Huder and Lee Kisling. Thank you for answering my big ask.

I need to give a heads up to Fluffy, our old cat, whose anguished howls of hunger got me out of bed early to start my day and my writing.

Most of all I need to thank my partner, Poet Ellen Lord, whose encouragement and excellent edits, kept me polishing my work until the finish. Thank you Ellen.

Edd Tury
July 9, 2024